THE DEADLANDS
FALL 2025

THE DEADLANDS

ISSUE 40, FALL 2025

© 2025 by Psychopomp. All Rights Reserved.

ISBN-13: 979-8-89116-018-7

Psychopomp.com

Publisher's Note:
No part of this publication may be reproduced, distributed, or transmitted in any form or by any means, including photocopying, recording, or other electronic or mechanical methods, without the prior written permission of the publisher, except in the case of brief quotations embodied in critical reviews and certain other noncommercial uses permitted by copyright law.

For more information, contact Psychopomp: ask@psychopomp.com

This publication is a work of fiction. Names, characters, places, and incidents either are products of the authors imaginations or are used fictitiously. Any resemblance to actual persons, living or dead, events, or locales is entirely coincidental.

Publisher: Sean Markey
Editor in Chief: E. Catherine Tobler
Poetry Editor: Nicasio Andres Reed
Social Media: Felicia Martínez
Art Director: inkshark
Nonfiction Editor: David Gilmore
Necromancer at Large: Amanda Downum
Copy Editor: Laura Blackwell
Copy Editor: Annika Barranti Klein
Designer: Christine M. Scott
Cover: *Golden Maze* by Carly A-F

The Deadlands is distributed quarterly by:
Psychopomp
PO Box 36
Woodbury, VT 05681

Subscriptions can be purchased at weightlessbooks.com. Individual issues can be obtained by joining our Patreon (with many deadly perks).
Join here: thedeadlands.com/patreon

Copyrights to all stories and illustrations are the property of their creators. The contents of this publication may not be reproduced in whole or in part without the consent of the copyright holder.

FALL 2025

GUEST FICTION EDITOR:

VAJRA CHANDRASEKERA

TABLE OF CONTENTS

Fiction

THE LAST MINUTE BEFORE THE ROOSTER CROWS

Malena Salazar Maciá

ROSENDO had no intention of raising roosters. He couldn't even be sure he liked them. He inherited them, like one inherits baldness after thirty or the habit of bringing out the small table on hot afternoons to play dominoes with his neighborhood friends. He took care of the animals because no one else in town was interested in them, and someone had to feed them after the crowing.

His father raised roosters. He didn't like them either. He raised them only because of what he called the "principle of tradition": if his grandfather raised roosters and his great-grandfather too, then roosters were here to stay in the family. However, Rosendo, who was born what he called "genetically exiled," studied mathematics in Havana.

He went far enough to believe he was convinced he wouldn't return to San Andrés, a town that Google Maps forgot. Nor was it well-known on the bus routes and other motorized transport, even old ones like the almendrones. It was only reached by tractors that survived the ten million harvests owned by one in twenty residents, or by horse-drawn cart, and sometimes even the horses got lost in the woods.

His thesis, "Topological models applied to fractal structures in the context of predicting microhistorical chaos," was never published. The university congratulated him on the day of his defense and asked him not to insist. Someone on the panel told him it was too poetic. Another, more sympathetic, asked if he couldn't do something more useful, like work in a winery.

Rosendo returned to the village when the news reached him. In the end, he concluded, one always returns to places one would rather forget. Sometimes due to illness, sometimes due to death, and sometimes due to a desire to disprove one's heritage. He arrived in town with a folder of unused equations and an ego wrapped in cellophane. The chicken coop was still there.

His father claimed that roosters were meat clocks. And that very thing killed him. A poorly programmed clock that didn't crow. From then on, the roosters stayed with Rosendo, who learned that everything that crowed broke something; sometimes a dream, sometimes twelve o'clock. Sometimes, they broke life.

His mother, asthmatic, lived in an epilogue. She never complained. She breathed with difficulty. She spoke very softly, almost silently, and classified things into two categories: "what's useful" and "what hasn't yet proven itself useless." Rosendo belonged to the latter.

"Are you going to take care of the roosters at last, or should we make a pot of soup for the town?" she asked him at their first dinner, when the boy hadn't even shaken the dust off the threshing floor.

"Yes. I'll take care of them. Until I find something else."

"Then make sure they crow."

Rosendo didn't understand a thing. The roosters always crowed. On time. At the wrong time.

Upon his return, he discovered that his mother had developed the habit of bottling her own air. She did it at dawn, before the dust closed in on her chest. According to her, it was a way of protecting herself.

"Mijo, this air I blow into the glass is mine, it's unique," she said. "No one else has used it. Virgin air, son. Like me before your father."

Rosendo found that, in addition to tending to the chicken coop, he had to help his mother organize the bottles on the porch. Some had labels written with a marker that had less ink left than gasoline in a rural tractor: *fresh air at 3:03 a.m., left lung with wheezing. 6:00 a.m., sigh of dissatisfaction for a son who didn't meet expectations. 2:18 a.m., air before the rooster, 4:00 a.m.*

Rosendo had serious doubts about his mother's practice. The bottles were empty. Once, secretly, he opened one with the note *Disappointment. 2:15 a.m.* He immediately felt a strong, hot slap which made him fall on his buttocks in the doorway. A good old-fashioned slap, the kind that would crush the nose if it hit in the face, just like the ones he received as a child when he went to the river without permission with his friends to cool off in August. From that day on, he gave up on opening bottles and let them multiply.

However, his mother's real warning came with Ciclón, Rosendo's first rooster of his own, reddish and half-witted. He didn't even know how to impregnate chickens. Every time he crowed with his tender hoarseness, someone ceased to exist.

At first, it went unnoticed. Olga never opened her guava bar shop again. A man who fixed radios disappeared from his window. The girl who brought them bread vanished like a bag carried away by the wind. Every time Ciclón sang, the town began to shrink.

Rosendo pointed this out to his mother.

"That's paranoia, mijo," she said, sealing the early morning air, classified as *the smell of onions between my teeth. 1:14 a.m.* "Here, everyone who leaves comes back in different forms."

A French tourist who appeared in town was the first to buy a bottle of air from Rosendo's mother. A pale man, with a face that had just emerged from a hole in the ground. Understandable, given that San Andrés was hard to find. He stopped in front of the doorway where Rosendo's mother was taking stock, asked about the bottles. The woman explained the contents and said he could try one. If he liked it, she would sell it to him at a good price.

The Frenchman, intrigued, uncorked one without any notes. Immediately, he cried out loudly. Between sniffles and sips, he stammered that it was art. In broken Spanish, he said: "Air with memory sells well."

Rosendo, who remained present at all times to prevent his mother from being scammed, said nothing when his mother confessed that she had breathed her childhood into the bottle. The Frenchman bought five more bottles. He paid fifty euros for each and left a cell phone number that was of little or no use in San Andrés. He never returned.

Meanwhile, Rosendo concentrated on Ciclón, on his random songs, on the townspeople who vanished like dandelions when the wind blew. He took out his old university notebook and began creating equations, solving for variables. He drew columns: *name, time of crow, missing, body found or not, atmospheric condition, Mom's breathing.*

It became an obsession for Rosendo, who stayed close to Ciclón as much as possible. Later, he created a model. Mathematics was impartial. It didn't create ghosts. Rosendo wondered if the rooster's crow was an algorithm programmed to erase people. Or if it wasn't the crow, but the silence that followed.

"That rooster crows in hexameters," his mother said one morning, while vacuuming in front of the entrance. She had created an entire community that bought her bottles. Many would bring her the first container they had at hand, and she had to hurry to expel all the air she had stored. "The country crows in prime numbers."

"And how do you know what a hexameter and a prime number are?" Rosendo asked her.

"Just like you know what it's like for a mother to bottle up her lungs for fear of dying."

Rosendo felt a lump in his throat. Because he had begun to believe, and this was the first time he felt doubt. Not of his mother, who was always strange, but of himself. Maybe he had imagined everything. Maybe there weren't any missing people.

He went to look for Olga. The house was boarded up. No one remembered buying guava bars there. He asked for the mechanic. A drunk told him there had never been radios in the town. He looked for the girl. They asked him which one he was talking about. The one with the bread, Rosendo clarified.

There was no answer. The guy selling coffee on a bicycle, who was passing by at that moment, stopped to ask if he was okay.

Rosendo went back to his notebook. He read the equations. They were perfect. There was beauty in the logic. Also, a bit of horror. One day after the hoarse sound of Ciclón at dawn, they found the body of Nando, the man who sold yuca in the pasture. On his skin was an equation written in blue ink: one of those Rosendo had created according to Ciclón's singing patterns. The police asked him if it was his, given that he was the only mathematician in town.

Before they broke into his house to look for the notebook or destroyed his mother's prosperous bottled air business, Rosendo confessed that it was his, but that it was also Pythagoras's, if you looked at it with goodwill. They didn't arrest him because the town was very small and crazy people caused trouble. It was enough to greet them with reservations.

And the second rooster in Rosendo's brood was born: Bendición, with a tomato-red comb, a golden breast, and a dark tail. He named him that despite the fear of what his first crow might provoke. Bendición's song was sweet, strong, and emotional, and even stranger than Ciclón's, it turned out: people returned every time he sang. Olga reopened her guava bar stand. When Rosendo visited her to ask what had happened, she claimed she had bought some air bottles and taken them to the neighboring town to sell, as a favor for Rosendo's mother.

The mechanic returned, and Radio Enciclopedia was playing in every house. The little bag of bread appeared hanging on Rosendo's doorstep after a song of Bendición, and he could see the girl with longer braids walking next to the man selling coffee. And people began to say that Nando, with a different equation written in black ink on his skin, was on the main road, with his little stand of yuca that fell apart at the sight of the pressure cooker.

Rosendo had another problem to solve, since Ciclón was disappearing people with his singing, and Bendición was returning them with implausible excuses.

"When you arrived here all Havana clad, I told you had to make sure the roosters crowed," his mother reminded him one morning while she was labeling her bottles. San Andrés, suddenly, was on Google Maps. Foreigners were coming to buy bottled air. Rosendo suspected the Frenchman. "This place almost got screwed!"

She blew into a plastic water bottle with the Ciego Montero label worn. She closed it quickly and wrote: *Finally, damn it. 1:19 a.m.*

However, Rosendo created new equations for Bendición. Sometimes he found patterns with Ciclón's. Parallels that anyone else would have ignored, but not him. He was determined to understand the mystery of the crowing of the roosters. He tried to intervene. He gagged Ciclón's beak, leaving him the bare minimum for a drink of water. Someone cut his rope. He gave him a drop of alcohol to make him faint. He resisted, such an idiot, and crowed anyway. In the rooster's moments of silence, which were more frequent than Bendición's, dawn took a very long time to arrive. People fled dazedly from their houses, arrived late to work, to the fields, and his mother had more time to expel the asthmatic air from her lungs to refill the bottles. Demand grew. Rosendo went to the town doctor, who looked at him like one looks at a bucket full of dirty water when he showed him the notebook and his theories.

"Hum, so, let's begin…Do you hear voices?"

"No. Only roosters."

"Yeah. Sure. Do roosters talk to you?"

"No! No way! How could a rooster talk? They don't have the appropriate vocal apparatus for…"

"I understand, of course. You need to understand that I'm just here to help you. H-e-l-p-i-n-g y-o-u."

"Doctor, why are you talking weird?"

"Weird? Not at all. So, back to the topic…And…do you think people die when this rooster…Lung …?"

"Ciclón. The reddish one."

"Yes, that one. Do you think people vanish when he crows?"

"I'm not sure. I don't know what to say. Because Bendición makes people come back. Exactly five days later, at six-thirty in the morning, according to my calculations in my notebook… you see? Is this equation…at that time, Bendición crows and the people return. They come back changed, but they come back."

"Then it's fine. If you are sure, if people come back, no matter if with one more or one less gray hair, then there is no problem."

After the consultation, Rosendo cloistered himself. He didn't speak to anyone, not even his mother, even though he heard her blowing into bottles every morning and the murmur of people in the doorway reached his room. The hens and roosters began to follow him even when he wasn't feeding them. They perched on his bedroom window like silent witnesses and stared at his notebook.

A new rooster had been born: Silencio. Soon he became Rosendo's shadow. He still hadn't crowed. It was impossible to create an equation for him, or to know what would happen when he sang his first note in the early morning. Rosendo was afraid. Ciclón made people disappear. Bendición brought them back. He wondered what Silencio would do.

So, one night, Rosendo entered the chicken coop and grabbed Silencio. He severed his vocal cords with a surgical precision that was unheard of, as if instead of studying mathematics, his future had been in medicine. The rooster looked at him with an ancestral sadness.

That night, it rained.

At dawn, Rosendo's mother wasn't there. He couldn't find her anywhere. The house was empty. He called her several times and received no response—not a scream, not a deep cough, not a wheezing, not a complaint, not a demand. He went to his mother's room and found the place covered in dust, as if years had passed without anyone using the bed. Rosendo ran to the front door to check the balance. Nothing. The porch was empty. There was only an unlabeled bottle.

Rosendo picked it up. It was warm. He hesitated. He opened it.

A warm breath hit his face. It sounded like asthmatic breathing. As if his mother were on the other side of the glass neck. It was a cough. Two, three times. And then, nothing.

From then on, Rosendo only cared about making sure Ciclón and Bendición sang. He cut the vocal cords of the rest of the roosters. And he feverishly immersed himself in creating equations to predict the next clutch, because roosters were meat clocks, and those too were perishable.

And in the early mornings, Rosendo bottled the air of his lungs at the last minute before the rooster crows.

Just in case.

Poetry

AMANITA SEASON

Belle Biscotti

Beneath the necrotic oak
the Death

Caps flourish their flesh-
umbrellaed skulls

in the inhuman hours
of the morning—

each a metabolic tomb
siphoning.

Multifoliate

despite the heaving, pulse-
less floor

these watchful doormen
of our final address

flattening their haunches
in the loam.

———————

Nine days old—

the doe's early pelt reflects
and drags

for the unfurling, crucial
nutrient strike:

Great Atrophy / spore
of decay / threshing eye-

let / silver gill.
The colony wants nothing

more in return.

Fiction

HAMAKA, LEAVE ME ALONE

Testimony Odey

LIKE A FUGITIVE thing transmorphing, you are alive with a sea of names. Bianonyerem. *Stay with me.* An impossible plea. Chimamanda. *My chi will never fail me.* It did. The Idibia had said to your mother the second time you were born: *"Even our personal gods respect destiny."* The third time you were born, your father's nostrils twitched as he inhaled the snuff on the back of his left palm in one swift motion. He was weary of spending so much on naming ceremonies that ended up inconsequential. Truly, why invite the whole village to celebrate the coming of a child who shared the same destiny with the sunset? Your mother turned you up and down in the dim flickering glow of the candle, her hands searching for a sign that you were a fragile evil thing reborn. A gentle lament slipped through her lips when she felt the healed gash on your right thigh. Managing to creep out of her hut, she raised you to the luminous, midnight sky, her teeth sunk into the tender softness of her lips, her tongue in crimson baptism and anointed you with a name. Hamaka. *Leave me alone.* But you were not one to follow orders. *Leave who alone?* The witching hour carried your sharp, piercing wails on its wings, until your tiny, delicate lips found your mother's darkened nipple, overflowing with milk.

The next day, the Idibia paid a visit to your father's house, his white wrapper tied firmly around his waist, his worn-out leather bag over his shoulders, his feet bare. He resembled a man who did not accept defeat easily, a handful of cowries entangled in those long-dreaded beards of his. It was not your first time seeing him. He had a habit of addressing your spirit each time you came into this godforsaken mortal world.

"Don't torment your mother so," he tried to cajole you into staying the first time you came. "You slip in and out of the door between the living and the dead like water in open fingers, but you must take pity on your mother. She has begged in every way that you stay with her: look at your name, look at the beautiful waist beads she made with her very own hands to adorn your waist, look at the tears in her eyes…"

The second time, he shook his head and asked for a knife.

"She might go again," he told your parents. "But I am making this mark on her right thigh so her blood can touch the earth. This way, she is bonded to mother earth and the next time she comes, she will stay longer."

This time, he chewed a chewing stick while staring at the heavens. The clouds, like white foam, veiled the sun's harsh rays. The breeze sang, rustling leaves, and the red sand in your father's compound shone. After minutes of chewing, he cleared his throat and lowered his eyes. His pupils seemed lost in a different world, although they were fixated on your parents.

"She must make a decision herself. Nobody can force her. She must choose whether she wants to be bound to a string of restless souls taking turns at life or if she wants freedom from it. It is a choice only she can make."

Finding your puffy cheeks with her thumb, your mother ran tired circles on them. In her eyes, you could see the sad resignation of a woman whose strength could never equal that of the gods. Your father waved off a fly.

"Can we, no matter how little, influence her choice?" he asked in his usual quiet baritone voice.

The Idibia chewed his plump, dark lower lip in thought and said with a shrug, "You can beg her."

"Please stay," your parents said in unison, and while you wanted to respond with *don't beg me,* you found yourself staring at your mother's swollen breasts whose milk would sour without suckle, her red eyes and frail heart. And while your father put on the air of a man unaffected, you could see the desperate rhythmic tapping of his toes, digging into the red earth as though trying to drill a hole. You squirmed in your mother's arms, like a worm trying to wriggle its way out of a terribly uncomfortable dilemma. *Hamaka, please stay,* she whispered. And your soul and spirit thought strongly of the liberation before you, felt deeply the need to honour the pact you made with mother earth in your last coming, and while you were uncertain of how long you would linger, you were sure of one thing: you would surrender to this blooming freedom and like your first name, stay.

I HAD A DREAM AND IN THE DREAM I KNEW I WAS DREAMING SO I BELIEVED I COULD CHANGE THINGS

Shana Ross

Bava Batra 121b

This could be a good day.

                    If?   If.

        If a whole generation stops dying.

Stops?

                    Finishes.   Completes the process.

We've all been waiting.

And the prophet tells it like this.

                    It happened: all the men of war

                    were consumed and dead.

Look – blessed is he   who is good   (and)   who does good.

                    Prayer in the form of a Venn diagram.

            Is there proof?   A proof: only

what we are promised.

        After the war,   we will be able   to bury the
dead.

Holy   holy   is the overlap.

Blessed is he   who honestly thanks   [god]   that there is a
body left

        to bury.   Blessed

is he who does the burying.

A handful   of dirt,   stones on   the mounding—

wash your hands,

      wash your hands,

           wash your hands of,

wash your hands until   you are clean enough

to return   home to the living,   to be
with the living, to walk

    alongside the living.

And this we will commemorate?   A good day. A good day.

Fiction

THE DESTRUCTION OF ALL THAT IS GOOD AND HOLY, OTHERWISE KNOWN AS GREEN BEANS

Erin Ulm

1. PROGRESS

The giant turtles walked out of the sea, clambering onto the dock's wooden slats. "We will survive on land, we will survive on land," they chanted in their distinct language, the turtle tongue. "We will, we will, we will."

The turtles did not like the sea any longer. "How salty!" they cried in disgust. "How terribly wet!" They figured themselves far too wonderful to be in the sea any longer. They wanted to feel the sun warm their shells always. They wanted humans to stare in awe at their magnificence, for they were the grandest of sea creatures, and feed them their meats and cheeses and green beans. They wanted to be feared; they wanted to be loved.

Yet some were afraid. "The ocean is all we know," they protested. And so the ambitious turtles began the chant to soothe the frightened ones.

"We will survive on land—only on land! We will survive on land—only on land! We will, we will, we will!"

And so the turtles walked grandly to the end of the dock, where sand met wood.

2. SMALL DOSES

"What are you hungry for?"

"Anything, really," the woman said, scratching her flaking elbows. "I haven't eaten in a while." She brushed a strand of hair behind her ear, slightly self-conscious.

The manager of Green Beans 'N' Foodstuffs, Inc. #10,302 smiled. "We have a fine selection of samples today. Green beans, dried jerky, potato soup."

The woman glanced at the sign to the right of the manager's desk. "Only in small doses," she read softly to herself.

"I'm sorry," the manager said, pushing her glasses up on her nose. "Seems everyone's hungry for something these days. We only have so much to go around."

The woman scratched more urgently at her elbows. "I understand. I'd like a green bean, please."

The manager turned promptly from the desk and went into the shadowy back of the room. The woman heard rummaging. When the manager came back, she held a single green bean in her hand. She offered it to the woman.

The woman took the bean with trembling fingers. "Just a morsel," she said to herself. "Just a little bean. But it's enough." She looked up at the manager as if for affirmation.

"Yes," replied the manager automatically. "It's enough. It's enough for every one of our customers. And it's only a half-ration, after all."

The woman's lower lip quivered. "Only half? Is that enough?"

"Yes. It's enough for everyone if you're strong-willed enough."

The woman nodded and tore the green bean in half. She dutifully handed one piece back to the manager, then nibbled the other.

"Is it good?"

"Yes. Very." The woman shook all over. She nibbled and nibbled and nibbled.

"I'm glad. We're all glad. Another satisfied customer," the manager murmured, writing something down on her clipboard. She then smiled brightly at the woman. "Next, please."

The woman, holding the green bean tightly, shuffled on her way and out the door. There was a long line ahead, every single person wanting for something. Always wanting.

The manager asked once more, "What are you hungry for?"

The little girl just blinked her eyes at the manager. "*For*," she said, tasting the word. She savored it like it was food. Like it was a green bean.

3. SHERRI AND THE MATRON

The girl's name was Sherri. She had very sharp teeth. These teeth were very good for swallowing others' words. Sherri swallowed these words because she was mute and had none of her own. Sharp teeth were the best at swallowing words because the fine tips could snag the ends of them as they passed by. Sherri hated the sound of others' voices, but she loved their words. There were so many of them it made her salivate. When Sherri swallowed words, they trumpeted back up her throat like half-chewed music notes, springing into the air, thin and melodious. The words didn't taste of anything, but Sherri'd feel a tingle in the back of her mouth when she caught one or two. Sometimes she was lucky to catch a whole sentence, if it was short. She'd usually only catch the last word of a sentence, as those were the slowest to disappear. The words were small and wispy, soft as silk.

When she didn't hear anyone's voices, or was too tired to catch any words, Sherri's throat grew unbearably sore and parched. It was a thirst no water could quench, and for that Sherri sometimes hated her strange talent of swallowing words. They were tasteless, but it was wonderful to feel them slide smoothly off her tongue.

Sherri lived in a crumbling house. The matron who owned the place was always wanting potato soup and green beans, so "potato soup" and "green beans" were common phrases Sherri repeated. The matron didn't mind Sherri's muteness as long as she wiped the mud off her feet coming in from the rain, watched out for "the horrible turtles," and went to bed on time.

4. CELEBRATION OF HUMANITY

Every day the robots worked in Town #0003. It was an unconscious kind of work. They cleaned their houses, dusted the windowsills, and made the beds. They peeped out windows and said, "Hello, how are you?" to each other. They went to offices and drank oil out of steaming mugs and waited for assignments. When they received assignments, they completed them in a timely manner. They swallowed dinners of nuts and bolts in the shape of green beans and drank wineglasses of greasy black oil. They kept streetlights up and working. They did everything right. Every morning was the same as the last. The sun rose, the sun set, again and again and again. The robots worked every day. They never rested. They were smooth and efficient and flawless.

They made amiable small talk and held deep, scholarly discussions of philosophy and the meaning of life. All the deep discussions were shallow, them being robots, but they tried their best anyway. Everything was nicely done. Every weather forecast was accurate due to advanced technology, though there wasn't any weather variation at all, so this was quite an easy feat. Every shop window went unmarred by the touch of human fingers. The streets were empty of all litter. Everything was done with a sense of punctuality. The television broadcast spectacular TV programs at all the convenient times of day. The robots were very good actors.

Books were solidly written, though none of them were classics in any sense of the word.

The robots worked and worked and worked until time turned everything to rubble, and all was perfect.

5. COMPANIONSHIP

"Goodbye!" the girl screamed to her parents from outside the crude little shack, leaning on the tips of her toes into the doorway. Her parents were very hard of hearing, almost deaf, because they had forgotten their SoundSomething Ear Things when everything happened, before she'd been born. Thankfully, they'd been far away when it happened—others were not so lucky.

Beside her floated a little gray box in the shape of a radio, tethered to her wrist by a thin colorless string. It crackled and hummed softly. The box had a scratched label on it that read MADE BY NEW 'N' IMPROVED ELECTRONIX #2,3000.

The girl left, walking down the long gravel slope of her driveway, sidestepping piles of ash and mangled pieces of furniture. When she leapt over a rotted leg of a queen-sized bed, the box bounced joyously beside her. The air was silent; it rolled over the girl and her companion in thick, sulfurous bursts. The girl wrinkled her nose at the smell. "What is that?" she asked.

The box paused before answering in a cool, pleasant female voice, "That information is restricted."

The girl pursed her mouth and rolled her eyes. They continued on their way. The girl stopped after a few moments to jab a finger at the gray, ashy sky. "Look at that," she demanded of her box. "Look at that! Smoke rings!"

The box didn't answer, just crackled quietly. The girl, disappointed, kept walking, yanking the box hard behind her.

"How are you doing?" asked the box serenely after a while.

"Okay," groused the girl, kicking at a piece of burnt wood.

"What was that?"

"Never mind."

At one point they happened upon the crumbled half of a building. The girl inspected the ruin meticulously, squinting, making faces at the bits of smoldering debris, the box drifting ever close. "Another piece of junk," the girl announced after she was finished. Then she turned to her companion. "What was this place?"

"A house," said the box simply.

"*Duh.* Did people live here?"

"Yes. Two people."

The girl's eyes widened. "What were their names?"

"Sheryl Winbatt and Ariel Swanson." The box's voice was calm as ever, but the girl paced back and forth, newly invigorated.

"Okay," she murmured. "That's good for a start. What happened to them?"

The box didn't answer. It hummed fuzzily.

"Answer me, you," said the girl. She grabbed the box from its perch in the air and shook it.

"Zzzzt," said the box. "That information is restricted."

The girl's face reddened. She muttered unintelligibly under her breath, kicked a chunk of a half-melted can of green bean mush, and left the house, dragging the box sullenly behind her.

The girl walked farther and farther. Occasionally she stopped to pluck pebbles out of the soles of her feet. "You know," she remarked after an hour of unbroken silence, "I feel like you hardly listen to me."

"You feel I don't listen to you?"

"Yes," said the girl impatiently. "That's what I just said. I feel like you just don't listen at all. I know my parents didn't put too many responses in you, but still. You're *supposed* to listen to me. That's what you're *for*." She kicked at the ground for emphasis. She was doing a lot of kicking today.

"I do listen to you," said the box calmly.

"You're so *stupid*!" burst the girl, whirling on the bobbing box in a rage. "I ought to smash you! You're useless! You don't tell me *anything*! Anything I *want* to know!"

The box sizzled tonelessly.

The girl's eyes glimmered. She kept walking, looking down at the ground. "I don't like you anymore," she muttered insolently, face an unattractive scarlet. "I try to talk and ask questions and you don't answer me, you don't answer me at all. I don't want you anymore. You're no *help*." Her lips puckered, face crumbling. "You're not even a good friend."

The box said, "I will do better."

"You can't. You're a machine."

"I will do better. I will—"

"You know, I have a little rock stuck in my foot." The girl's eyes were filled with trembling upset. Her heart throbbed. She couldn't catch her breath. The rock stung badly.

"It's *stabbing* at my *heel* and you didn't even *know*!" the girl shouted shrilly into the empty, gray air, eyes wild. "You're *supposed to know*! That's what you're for! That's why you're here! You're supposed to know what's *wrong*!" She began to blubber, eyes wetly streaming. "I ask you every day! *Every day*! And you don't help me, you don't even know how! You're supposed to know, but you *don't*! You're broken!"

"I am entirely functional. I will do better," said that calm, smooth voice. "I will do better."

The girl wiped her eyes on her sleeve. "Then tell me what happened."

"What happened to what?"

"What happened to—to—everything."

The world went silent.

The box crackled, all noise and static.

"Well?" the girl snapped.

"I will do better. I will do better. I will do better," the box buzzed. It would not stop. It was stuck. "Please. That information is restricted. Zzzzt."

The girl went home. There was nothing left to do. She limped as she went—the pebble was still stuck in her heel.

6. A FABLE FROM A TATTERED AND SOOTY CHILDREN'S TEXTBOOK

There was an unduly large crow sitting in the middle of Town #40,789, and Henry, the manager at the local Green Beans 'N' Foodstuffs, Inc. #60,889, was the only one who noticed at first simply because he often counted his money in the very same place the crow perched. The crow watched the smoky pollution in the air with its beady eyes, and Henry watched it.

The crow didn't move much—it flapped its dark wings a little, shifted its position slightly, but overall it seemed to be concentrating on something Henry couldn't see. He could sense the dewy bright intelligence in its eye. Henry wanted desperately to capture it.

Henry left the crow only for an instant to grab his lasso from the shed, but the moment he returned to the square a small crowd had gathered. A working-class woman had fainted dead away and was lying, still in her apron, on the floor. Her sister was gabbing away with the local judge, who was eyeing the crow severely.

"It's going to steal our green beans!" insisted Henry in a powerful voice. "Be sensible, people! How can we let it stay?"

"Yes! We need to save the beans! And what if it pecks out the eyes of our children?" gasped the schoolteacher of P.S. #40,789.

"We have to save the green beans, yes," said the owner of the Miscellany Shop #40,789. "Yet it's only sitting there. Perhaps it's just having a rest and then it will fly away." The judge nodded in slow, measured agreement.

"Someone take a picture!" yelled a working-class housewife from the back of the crowd, and suddenly all were pushing forward to get a better glimpse.

"Stand back, everyone. I'll get the beastie," said the owner of New 'N' Improved Electronix #40,789.

"Don't hurt it!" begged his small daughter at his side, tugging on his leg. "Maybe it's a baby bird."

"A baby? That big?" wondered the housewife.

"I say we call the authorities," barked her husband.

Henry pushed his way through the crowd. He readied his lasso, swirled it above his head, and let it fly around the crow's neck. He was determined to save the green beans.

The bird's head swiveled to look at Henry the moment the rope touched it. Simultaneously, an enormous explosion occurred in Town #3000. The townsfolk ducked, slamming their hands to the sides of their heads in agony. Blood spurted and leaked from their ears in terrible streams, pooling on the cobblestones. Henry dropped the rope in surprise and pain, collapsing to the floor. All the townsfolk died. They had all forgotten their earplugs in the middle of all the excitement.

MORAL: Disaster can occur at any time. Be prepared with SoundSoft Earplugs—"If On Dying You're Not So Keen, Save Your Family & Green Beans!"™

7. "THE BEAN OF GREEN": A SHORT SOLILOQUY

"Green beans, green beans!" the actress screams loudly so as to reach her imagined listeners, her face white with powdery ash, the smears of artfully applied blood on her plump cheeks flaring bright. Her ears are twisted into unrecognizable lumps of flesh.

She stumbles forward on the blackened wooden board she uses for a stage, imaginary spotlight warming her many-pimpled back. She is naked, red with splotches. "Tell me, what were they like?" Her face is abominably wishful, eyes glistening poignantly at the empty landscape before her. "I cannot remember. Forgive me, it has all slipped away. Were they truly green? As green as the fields? Were they earthly things? They must be, for beans are as earthly as any of us. Grown from the soil, grown from Mother Earth, like potatoes for our soup? Were they sweet? Is it ungodly, unholy, to ponder the taste?" Her face slips smoothly into a grave, grim expression, surveying the gray landscape. "Is it ungodly?" she repeats in a thundering voice, eyes fervent.

She paces across the stage in a fit of anxiety and wonder. "I believe it is and I believe it isn't. Who am I to dare to contemplate such things? But still, I contemplate." Her face grows perilously soft. She straightens her back and stares at nothing.

"I can't help myself," she says quietly, tragically, eyes wide, face pale and waiflike as the moon. "I wonder, I wonder—" She raises her great, resounding voice to the invisible rafters and cries, rapturously, "Were they green? Green as the horrible turtles? Or—*oh!*—were they green as heaven?"

Nonfiction

THE RITUAL

Matthew Wollin

THE RED EARTH from my grandmother's graveyard stained my white sneakers. I wiped it off later, with a damp paper towel, crouching in my parents' laundry room while my brother and parents were all busy elsewhere. I had imagined doing it in the middle of the night, in the dark, after everyone else was asleep, but each time I had forgotten or fallen asleep myself first, and so it only happened when I finally needed to wear those sneakers back to my apartment in the city several days later, and by then it was daytime and bright.

That whole time those shoes had sat unnoticed in the laundry room with the edges of their soles darkened, almost indistinguishable from their normal dirt and grime. The paper towel came away red when I pressed. I needed two to get it all off. I am wearing those shoes now as I write. Is it strange that I wish they were still stained?

My father reached for my hand, which I can never remember having happened before. She was his final parent to die. The size of the coffin: I could see it all and imagine her inside of it, and the fact that it could contain her was strange, because when a person is alive the body seems less like a container and more like an expression; but this was just a container.

The coffin teetered just briefly as it was drawn out of the hearse, and the lid lifted a fraction of an inch, but I could not see anything. I wish I had gone with my aunt to identify the body.

What is the feeling I am trying to capture?

The problem with death is it makes everything trite. Everyone has had the experience, and so there is nothing left for you to write that has not already become a cliché. I think that is why it is better to default to a person's faults when remembering—the charming ones at least, if we do not wish to be rude. My dad did well with that at the eulogy. Yet even that was too pat.

The juxtaposition, the question that I keep coming back to, is whether my grandmother is gone or not. Whether she is in fact contained in that box beneath the red earth that we threw on her body one by one with the same shovel in the Jewish cemetery, visions of *Schindler's List* dancing like sugarplum fairies all through my head, or whether she was whatever she left behind that is not in that box. Perhaps that is the purpose of the box: to make it clear that everything outside the box is still here.

Where does the ritual end?

The notification upon my return from vacation that my grandmother had had a small stroke; the need of my parents to afford me my enjoyment in Argentina; the reassurance that she was still all right even after. The checking in day by day, and then her having another, more significant stroke; was the stroke a part of the ritual too? Not knowing when the end would come and having to be told by my boyfriend that I should go to see my parents at once despite the uncertainty, my chronic self-centeredness. The fact that I no longer regard that self-centeredness as a flaw but a fact. Deciding what to put in my bag when I went, unsure if I should bring a suit, and deciding not to, but to wear a neutral outfit at least. A dark one, except for the shoes; I do not have good comfortable dark shoes that are warm. Arriving at my parents' house to find only my mom, my dad in New Jersey with my grandmother; he would be there until she had breathed her last breath. The notification that she had, that my father had watched, he and his sister both, the two of them only; is it strange I am happy for them? I hugged him when he came in, really hugged him, not just the token normal one. Thinking about it now, I wanted to stay there for longer. I was afraid to stay there for longer because he would think that I needed it; but I did. Why was I scared? His tone as he told us about it, his strange, normal tone in which he describes everything, "it is what it is," "that kind of a thing," my irritation with it then immediately suppressed. Why was I irritated? No reason: because I was his child; because I still am.

We had sushi for dinner that night. The next morning I found out that my brother, who was at the end of a long trip abroad for work, would be able to make it back for the funeral the following day, taking two flights overnight from Rwanda to La Guardia, which relieved me somewhat because I had been worried he might not forgive himself if he did not manage to be there; his sense of obligation has always been so strong. I didn't know if I should call it a funeral, or service, or memorial. I have not looked up the difference and will not. I slept poorly that night and every night thereafter that week, not because of my grandmother but because I overeat when visiting my parents: I stuff cheese and crackers and whatever else I can find into my mouth late at night and then lie down on the too-firm bed and feel like my midsection is solid rock no matter which way I turn and then sleep.

I slept poorly and then drove down with my mother the next morning, following my father, who had already gone to pick up my brother. My mother drove, which was a mistake; then I drove, which was also a mistake. I got out after parking at my grandmother's retirement home, finally, needing to walk around in a circle in the sun and breathe slowly to decompress. My mother will read this and focus only on any part that portrays her unkindly; I love you, Mom, and think the world of you, please do not worry.

I did not hug my brother, which was reassuring, because we never hug; we do not need to. We know what we mean to each other. I love him. I am growing sentimental as I write this, realizing it is because of my grandmother; or perhaps that is just me. But me is also her in a more indirect way; I am from her, and she was a warmhearted but unsentimental person, and this is how that now manifests in me.

I went inside the retirement home, and met my aunt, and cousin, and her husband, and made conversation and caught up, which was nice and was awkward in exactly the same measure as always. We waited for the ninety-six-year-old priest whom my grandmother liked and who would be saying a few words at the service to arrive; my father and aunt had chosen him instead of some, and I quote, "rent-a-rabbi," despite the priest's obvious lack of Jewishness, because he knew her in life, and the two of them liked each other; it was the right choice. He did a good job at the graveyard, after we all had parked in our myriad cars in the driveway that ran through the modest cemetery from which you could still hear the cars speeding by on one of the nearby highways that compose the north Jersey landscape; people were crying. I was not. I helped carry the coffin. After the priest spoke, my father did, and I was the tiniest bit worried it would rhyme (don't ask), and prepared myself to forgive him if it did, but thankfully it did not; he spoke of her foibles first and then her nice parts after. I liked the foibles especially. Those felt like her; they took this act out of the realm of the general and they made it specific, while the gravediggers politely waited across the driveway in their sweatshirts, chatting out of earshot; what a strange job that must be. Good for you, I thought in their general direction; those must be extremely well-adjusted people. Or perhaps spectacularly ill-adjusted ones; but these ones seemed nice. They were all men; are there female gravediggers? There must be, what a strange thought; now there's a glass ceiling no one is talking about. My mom and I left her pocketbook with the car keys in my dad's car accidentally afterwards, and had to wander the cemetery for ten minutes while he and my brother returned the priest to the retirement home and then came back to save us.

There was a pizza restaurant where everyone went for lunch, which had pictures of classic Hollywood bombshells in pinup poses pasted all around the urinal, seemingly encouraging inappropriate behavior; my mother told us later that the women's had the same thing but inverted, with shirtless men staring at her from black and white vistas while she peed. My extended family posed for a picture after lunch, which was a strange thing to do, but no less strange than not doing it. Now there is a picture of my father's family and my aunt's all together, smiling in this pizza restaurant an hour after we buried my grandmother. The earth was so red. My earth-stained shoes are blocked by a table in the photo. My brother and I drove back to my parents' together afterwards, and then all of us spent all of the next two days together, more or less. It was good; it was important; it was extremely normal. The second night together we watched the movie *Eileen*. It wasn't bad; it was missing something.

I took a Steuben crystal penguin that had been my grandmother's back to Brooklyn and put it in the cupboard, next to my wineglasses, because I liked the idea of it living there like a little secret; I did not send a picture of its location to my family the way my brother did with the mezuzah that had been my grandmother's and which he put on the door to his office, because I knew that someone would ask why I did not put it in a more prominent place, and I did not feel like answering. I had tried, briefly, putting it on a table in my living room; but it was wrong there. It was the wrong ritual; it was the wrong monument. Not the penguin itself, but the penguin in that location; it was not the way my grandmother fit into my life. I don't know why, I don't know. It was too static, I think. When I kept it in the cupboard next to the wineglasses it became a ritual again, a shrine to which I may pay homage not by lighting incense or making offerings, but by drinking wine, something whose quality and enjoyment is already inextricable from its provenance; it made this ordinary and enjoyable activity into a remembrance in a way that I did not mind. It felt right to me, for me. I don't know. Then I went to the gym and bought a sandwich, and realized at some point around there that I wanted to wake up the next day and write this.

I woke up the next day and I wrote, slightly uncertain at first, but did not waste time on the uncertainty, moving ahead anyway; and then I went back home afterwards. I bought groceries, about seventy dollars' worth, which seemed like a lot but also somehow is not; it is just what I needed after not being in my place for a week and then also pickles.

The next day was my birthday. Went to my birthday dinner with friends, a small selection, the ones with whom I always look forward to spending indefinite amounts of time individually, was how I described it to them. Ignored the remnants of the cold I had been fighting off from getting my mouth too close to the karaoke mic (do not sing Billie Eilish, I learned, her songs are lovely but too soft for karaoke), and drank slightly too much but not *too* too much wine. I woke up the next morning slightly bleary but not terrible, and if you are not going to drink a reasonable overmuch at your self-arranged birthday dinner four days after your grandmother's funeral, really when are you going to drink?

I took Sunday off; from what, you ask: from everything. Did nothing, I tried to do nothing; perhaps texted my friend with whom I have sex sometimes to see if he wanted to have sex; my lover had been out of town for too long, and I needed a release.

I woke up on Monday, which was the second-to-last week at my job; I had given notice five days before my grandmother died, after she had had her second stroke and I had known it was imminent, but I was not going to let a little thing like my grandmother's death disrupt quitting. Did actual work—work for money I mean—because they were still paying me, and it wasn't terrible, and was made even less terrible by knowing that I would not have to do it for much longer. I pitched pieces in between; neither of the pitches I sent out that week were an immediate success but neither were they immediate failures either, which is the way things go in reality—I was finally learning, after thinking for most of my life that if success was not immediate then it did not count as success, that success truly belonged to those who knew how to capitalize on early marginal successes. That will not fit on a T-shirt.

The weeks passed; I left my job at long last. My lover returned; I went to see him before he returned from DC, see his body and the play he was in, feel his body against mine, in mine; both of us had missed it, desperately. I had never missed someone else's body the way I missed his; never fantasized about someone I was already with the way that I fantasized about him, about things that we already have. He returned a week after my visit. It had been two months. And I was free, and he was free, and somehow, at nearly forty I was at last living the unmoored artist life that I always had dreamed about when I was younger but on different terms entirely, with a stack of mostly self-earned money in the bank that meant my life as an artist was anything but starving; I thought of my grandmother again. Not because of the crystal penguin next to the wineglasses, which did make me think of her a little every time I drank; but because I wondered to what extent the strange freedom I was feeling had to do with her being gone. It did not have much to do with it, I think, but it was hinting at the greater loss and freedom which I was approaching at some point in the medium-distant future, when my parents followed suit and then I would be on my own, at last, an orphan well past middle age. I fantasized about it; less than I had when I was younger, in truth; but I now acknowledged more openly those earlier fantasies of freedom, the fantasies of the greatest and most significant set of guardrails around my being finally being removed. I hated myself for the fantasy.

I got married; it was the happiest day of my life. Talk about another instance where the general overwhelms the specific and we succumb to cliché, sheesh. Every day with him was the happiest day; every time I was with him all the relentless whispering in the back of my head fell silent, no more connections to the past present future imagined fantastical except for the ways that they manifest in the person I was in that moment.

There was a ten-minute pause between the previous sentence and this one; I got lost in the reminiscence for a moment, or the imagining; is that muscle the same?

My mother died at last when I was in my sixties. It was so much different than I had anticipated; I was so much different than I had anticipated. It turns out that being thirty-seven does not prepare you for being sixty-four in any particular way. In the supremest of ironies, my father outlived her, despite her extreme health-consciousness, all of us gathering to say goodbye to her in a strange echo of my grandmother from all those years ago. I remembered not to wear white shoes. The earth was not red. It was me and my husband, my brother and his wife and their child, which they have had at long last, turning her into a grandmother just barely, but barely was all that she wanted; and my father, who could not stand on his own, floated in his mobile, eyes red, protesting that he was fine, but not as resistant to feelings as he used to be. He was not fine; he was maybe fine. I cannot imagine what he was in that moment. It is hard to look at him, it is hard to not look at him; I look at the ground, at the dirt and the grass, and realize all of a sudden that all this is wrong, that my mother did not wish to be buried but cremated; and the scene changes. We gathered elsewhere; where will she want her ashes to be spread? On the lake, I think, and if that does not turn out to be the actual truth, it is close enough, it will suffice. That is where we gathered, on the edge of the lake, which is serene, painted with the blue of the skies all above, fringed with the green and brown of early spring. My brother did it, and thankfully that thing that is always happening in movies where a gust of wind comes at the last minute and blows the ashes all over everyone's faces did not happen. She was a slowly spreading circle of ash in the water, floating for what felt like too long, a nearly uncountable number of minutes, until the edges finally became waterlogged, and she sank. It is difficult to write about; it is difficult to watch. There had been a long lead-up to this point; I was grateful for that time to prepare, but nothing can really prepare you for the unavoidable awareness that you will be the next generation to go. I hoped that in death she found some of the peace that always seemed to elude her in life; that she was proud of me at last. I can hear her protesting even now, she was proud of me already; I know, Mom. We arrived back at my parents' house, which they had been planning to vacate for the last fifty years without making good on that promise; I took off my shoes and put them just where I did when my grandmother died.

That night, while my husband was asleep, I went back downstairs and picked up the shoes and took a paper towel and wiped the dirt off them gently. There was a noise; my brother's child was standing there and watching; he asked me what I was doing. *Cleaning,* I told him; *Do you want something to eat?* He was not a child anymore—he could not have been—too many years had gone by; but I cannot help imagine him as one, it is already stretching the limits of my imagination to imagine him at all, to imagine any of this happening, and so forgive me if I stall him in eternal childhood; he wore the pajamas that I wore as a child in that house, they had Aladdin on them and they glowed in the dark. We ate crackers together, tears on my face not then but now as I write; eventually I told him, *Enough,* and put the crackers away and brought him back to his room, the guest room. My brother and his wife in my brother's childhood room, and me and my husband in mine, my father in what used to be my mother's office on the ground floor because he could no longer make it up the stairs. I turned away from my sleeping husband and went to my parents' room and looked at the now-empty bed. Sat where my mom used to sit and fell asleep with the light on like she did—

—and then it is my turn. I do not know who is there, I do not have it in me to imagine it. It has taken a lot from me to imagine this much already, but it needed to be taken. There I am on my bed, eyes cloudy, rheumatic, and ready to die because finally my faculties degenerated to the point where I could no longer write. Until that moment I was fine; my degenerating memory did not stop me from writing, nor did my joints, nor my body, there are many ways to overcome those things and record words these days; but something happened in the last month or two, and the writing no longer makes sense, I simply do not understand how the words fit together, and once that ability is gone I no longer understand the point of living. My husband is there, or he is not but he feels like he is; I can see him looking at me with all the love that has always been in his eyes, still there, stronger than ever; and I relax because I know that no matter how far I go I will not be alone, because part of what I am is the relation between us, and that relation exists whether he is there or not, and so wherever I go, he will go too. And it occurs to me now that he is not the only person with whom I have that relation; that, even if more complicated, even if I take it for granted, there is that distinctness of relation with all the other people I have kept in my life; that what I am with them is the space in between. I feel so sure of this: I feel sure that I have lived my life in such a manner that these relations exist.

This is the story I tell myself; these are the stories we tell ourselves; the fact that this one is fictional does not mean it is any less real. The stories finally overwhelm whatever is left of the unstoried me, and I am breathing my last breath, and then all that is left is the ritual, but this is my ritual and I am back where I started: I do not know how to love you, Grandma, without loving myself. I miss you.

Fiction

THE GHOST OF CERRERA ORBITAL STATION MAKES HERSELF KNOWN

Laila Amado

THE GHOST has always been here. You just didn't notice her before. She is in the whomp-whomp-whomp of the air pumps. In the thunk-thunk-pomp of the waste disposal system. In the blip-blip-blip of the navigational proximity alerts. In the low growl of engines, holding the station up in orbit above the dying Earth.

She is in the scrape of white chalk on the blackboard in the station's classroom. In the excited squeals of young students getting their first assignment right. In the voices echoing up and down the many hallways of this cosmic ark. In the songs survivors of the planet's demise teach their space-born children.

She is in the blinking lights of dashboards. In the fluorescent green of emergency path illuminators stretching along the patched-up floors. In the endless rows of numbers rolling down the screens of the command deck. In the blaring of alarm sirens. In the thump-thump-thump of the boots of emergency team workers, running towards another unfolding crisis.

She is in the whoosh of gas escaping from the pressurized tanks in the station's heating system. In the scalding milk of the hot white fog. She is in the hands of a woman helping you pull down the lever stuck in its upward position. In the faded ink of tattoos stretching over the taut muscles of her arms. In the rolled-up sleeves of her green overalls. "Some of us are dead, but we keep the station going," she says and smiles, before the white vapor swallows her whole.

She is in the warm scent of cinnamon wafting from the station's kitchens. In the rich red of tomatoes ripening in the greenhouses on Level Eight. In the crisp, clean sheets you fold into neat squares during laundry duty. In the warm sting of water in the power showers after a long shift.

She will be in the angry hiss of air escaping from the cracked faceplate of your EVA suit when the hull breach sends a broken pipe propelling into your head. Beyond the torn metal of the open rip in the station's wall, the stars will shine bright, as distant and indifferent as ever.

When you turn over and crawl towards the breach, she will crawl with you. When you lift yourself off the floor, she will rise with you. When you stand and patch that rip up—even if you can no longer hear the air escaping, even if you no longer see the stars—she will stand with you, and together you will keep the station going.

Fiction

THE PRETENDIAN

Jason Pearce

THERE IS NO MAGIC without the procedure. Three steps, each as important as the other and beautiful in their simplicity. But simple things are easily forgotten after so many years. And with each phase of your existence, the remembering gets harder.

Last time, you vowed to never forget again. You'd rehearse the steps in your mind as you walked the streets, muttering instructions under your breath lest you be overheard and found out.

Life has a way of taking over the vulgar business of existing. You develop an entitlement to the story you tell. Days, weeks, and months pass without so much as a thought for the procedure. Until you wake up old and muddled, with only a vague sense of how to prepare for the next transition.

Then, when all seems lost, muscle memory takes over.

And the procedure finds you again.

———————

"Good news, Mister Whiskeyjack. Your bloodwork is normal. No diabetes."

"That makes no sense," Leroy says.

"Your sugar levels are perfect," Dr. Simpson replies. "I can put you through a morning of needle jabs and peeing into a cup, but the results won't change."

"But I'm native. Diabetes is endemic to my people."

"You heard me call this good news, right?"

"Everyone in my family has it."

"Not everyone, apparently. Was your Dad diabetic?"

Leroy is drawing a blank. The memory lapses have been getting worse, but how can he not remember his own father?

"Yes," he lies. "Type 2."

"And your mother?"

"Same as Dad." Technically this is correct. Leroy is blanking on Mom, too.

"You're one of the lucky ones," says Dr. Simpson. "Keep eating right and exercising, and you should stay that way."

Leroy eases himself down from the examination table and reaches for his jacket.

"One thing I don't get," he says. "If my bloodwork is normal, why am I so tired all the time?"

Dr. Simpson looks up from his computer terminal and shrugs with his eyebrows.

"Age catches up on us, Mister Whiskeyjack. Our energy levels wane, we start forgetting where we left our keys—"

Leroy's ears radiate heat as he processes that last part.

"So, memory lapses are normal?"

The doctor's smile looks forced instead of reassuring. He rises from his chair and taps a wall poster showing a cutaway of the human brain, his finger encircling a purple-shaded swirl northeast of the nasal cavity.

"Normal to a point," the doctor says. "This seahorse-shaped structure is the hippocampus. There's one on either side, and they control memory. We still don't understand them 100 percent, but this much is certain: anything can mess up those little seahorses. Age is the most common culprit."

Leroy wasn't always old and bordering on senile. He even had a girlfriend, once. Girlfriend seemed like an odd word choice—they were well into their sixties at the time—but they never lived together, and Sandra found the word partner too businesslike. So girlfriend it was.

Sandra ran the microfiche room at the State Archives. Like the patrons who lined up at her desk each day, she was obsessed with genealogy. Sandra carried a ledger-sized print-out of her family tree and would tell anyone who'd listen that she was half Scottish, three-eighths Dutch, and one-eighth African American. She didn't identify as Black, though. Sandra knew better than to assume an identity based on distant ancestry.

When the commercials started coming on TV saying they could trace your DNA back ten generations, Sandra was all over it. The results corroborated her research, with percentages instead of fractions. Of course, Sandra couldn't be satisfied with just her own results. She insisted Leroy try it, too.

"What's there to find?" Leroy asked. "I was born on the Reservation, so I'm Lakota."

"You never know until you try," Sandra said. "Maybe a passing trader or dashing, young cowboy snuck in there somewhere."

"It's a waste of money."

"I'll pay for it," Sandra said. "All you need to do is swab your mouth."

Leroy's results came back in less than a month. The sealed envelope sat on his side table for three days before Sandra came over and snatched it up.

"You didn't tell me your results came in."

"You didn't ask."

"Aw! Were you waiting for me to open them with you?"

"Sure," Leroy said. "Let's go with that."

"A drum roll, please." Sandra tore off one corner of the envelope and slid a lacquered fingernail into the gap. It made a surprisingly good letter opener. A frown overtook her face as she began reading.

"Well, that can't be right."

"What?" Leroy asked.

"It says you're 50 percent West European and 50 percent unknown DNA."

Leroy held his bronze arms out in front of his body. "Do I look European to you?"

"What the hell is unknown DNA?" Sandra asked. "They're supposed to have coverage for every Indigenous tribe in North America."

"Told you it was crap," Leroy said.

"Maybe we should test again. What do you think?"

"I think we should break up," Leroy replied, opening the door.

STEP 1: THE HEART

Reaching a human heart is tricky and prone to beginner mistakes. You are eager, and with so little practice after six decades, you could be forgiven for trying to go through the breastbone. It seems like the most direct route, sawing upward through bone, an incision from bellybutton to chin like the door flaps on a tipi. Then jimmy the blade back into the ragged seam dividing what remains of the sternum, the handle serving as a lever as you open the gap enough for prying fingers to reach in, first from one side, then the other. You imagine the rib cage spreading, a shopkeeper's cabinet offering its wares.

You don't have time for this drama. Hacking through bone would be laborious enough with proper sawing instruments and impossible with this ancient, straight-edged blade. And you must act fast to reach the prize while it still beats.

The correct method is this: A single thrust with the blade parallel to the ground, piercing the body three inches below that troublesome breastbone. Then pull hard to the right—your right, which is the prey's left. Then plunge your free hand through the skin, fat and other warm, quivering goo, dodging lesser organs the way a driver weaves around potholes. Follow the pulsing rhythms until you hold that beating heart in your palm. Wrap your hand around the thrumming mass as best you can and await Step 2.

"Sir! Are you alright? Do you need help?"

Leroy finds himself standing at a supermarket counter. A loaf of white bread and two pounds of bacon sit on the conveyor belt in front of him. A paper coupon with a picture of the same bacon is wedged between the shrink-wrapped packages.

"Is there someone we can call for you?" asks the woman in the A&P smock.

"No," he says. "Just need to collect myself."

Leroy's hand gravitates to the breast pocket of his windbreaker, where it finds a wad of paper. He unfolds the yellowed sheet and recognizes his own ornate cursive.

> *Urgent note to self:*
>
> Your name is Leroy Whiskeyjack. You are a full-blooded Lakota and indirectly descended from Tasunke Witco, popularly known as Crazy Horse.
>
> You were born in 1938 on the Pine Ridge Reservation in South Dakota. Your parents were Norman Whiskeyjack and Grace Medicine. Norman was Chief of your tribe for twelve years. You were the first Native American to receive a PhD from Dennison University and are renowned for the Indigenous lens you cast on European history.
>
> You are reading this because you've reached the age where things slow down and memory fails you. Hang on, Leroy. Just a little longer and you move to the next phase of your existence.
>
> Good luck!
>
> Leroy

"Hey Chief, can you move it along? Some of us have lives to get back to."

Leroy looks up from the letter just in time to catch some serious stink eye from a sandy-haired man in a tailored suit. The man brandishes a bag of Spanish onions as though it were a human heart awaiting transplantation.

"Sorry." Leroy pats his pockets, still grasping the letter. The only thing he finds is his bus pass in a worn plastic sleeve. No wallet or loose change. He frowns at the cluster of groceries on the conveyor belt, then forces a sheepish grin for the clerk.

"I'll need to leave this for another day," he says. "Do you know where the bus stop is?"

Twenty-three-year-old Leroy had never tried alcohol before but felt he'd earned the right, no matter what mother used to say. He would stop at one, pouring the evening's budget into a single dram of what Professor Turcotte called "the good stuff."

"You have to celebrate," Turcotte said over the phone. "You beat a lot of people for this fellowship. I suggest a barrel-aged single malt."

The pub surprised him with its array of sparkling bottles on the shelf above the beer taps. Leroy sat on the stool closest to the door and attempted eye contact with the bartender, a tall, redheaded man who looked like he should be wearing a kilt.

"Lemme guess," the bartender said. "Beer?"

"I was hoping for something fancier," Leroy stammered. "Scotch, maybe?"

The bartender shook his head. "Nothing stronger than beer for Indians. Bar policy."

"Christ sakes, Willie. Give the young man what he asked for. And put it on my tab."

Leroy turned to see an old white guy who looked like he was still growing into his three-piece suit. His green irises caught the light as he winked at Leroy.

"Pour him an Ardbeg Seventeen," he commanded. "And one for me as well."

Willie bit his lip and turned to the wall of bottles.

"Sure thing, mister."

"That's very kind," Leroy said, "but I have money."

"Of course you do," said the old man.

Leroy blushed. "We don't even know each other."

"Strangers are just friends who haven't met yet." The old man extended a wizened hand. "Name's Henry King. Tell me all about yourself, my young native friend. What is your story?"

This is the part Leroy struggles with. He could remember a lot more clearly if he put what was left of his mind to it, but something in his gut tells him not to. It starts with the spindly old man named Henry King waving to Willie the bartender. "Keep the tab open. My new friend and I are going outside for a smoke."

Leroy didn't smoke back then and still doesn't, to this day. He can't remember why he followed Henry King into the alley. Polite gratitude for the old man's hospitality, perhaps? Or something about blowing tobacco smoke up to the open skies, the way Leroy's ancestors used to, instead of turning the air inside the bar a sickly grey blue. Either way, he remembers only the darkness of the alley, as though every star in the sky had taken the night off.

Leroy sees that darkness now, and the usual deep breathing exercises do nothing to shut out the memories. The cold bone handle of a knife as he wraps his hand around it and slips it from his pocket. The surprised flicker of eyes in the dark, timed perfectly with the tearing sound as the knife plunges through fabric and flesh. The choking sounds as the knife digs under the ribs, puncturing a lung, severing arteries. And the smell of blood, fresh and metallic through blackness.

Then nothing for a while, not even darkness. The memory resumes with Leroy walking back into the pub. He caught Willie's attention right away as he slapped a hundred-dollar bill on the bar.

"This is from the old man. You can keep the change."

Willie's eyes widened as he took the hundred-dollar bill and punched open the cash register. Leroy half expected him to hold the bill up to the light, checking for signs of counterfeit. Instead, he cashed out his tip and stuffed it into the hip pocket of his jeans.

"There's nothing else I can get you?" Willie asked.

"Actually," Leroy said, "do you have a pen I can borrow? And a piece of paper?"

STEP 2: EYE CONTACT

This part should be easy, but the timing is delicate. You must show your true form at just the right moment. Show it too early, before the light goes out of their eyes, and their last memory will be the sight of you, tendrils out, teeth menacing. As though your hand grasping their heart isn't bad enough. You do not want that.

Move too late, and the sea horses will have begun dying. That's even worse.

For Step 2, nothing less than perfect precision will do.

The one constant is eye contact. You lock onto their gaze and stay there. And as their eyes lower, so do yours. Resist nothing. Let the darkness take you. The magic will tell you where to go next.

Leroy catches himself dozing on the bus. He would have slipped into deep sleep and found his geriatric ass in some far-flung corner of the city, but the French Indian saves him.

Sometimes when Leroy is sleeping, this guy speaks French in his head. Either that or English with a French accent. Neither of which makes sense. Leroy has never been to Quebec, much less France, and French 101 was the only course he didn't ace in undergrad. The man's voice rasps through darkness, intense and imploring, using words that escape Leroy as he bolts upright in bed, drenched in sweat. He never remembers the man's face, but something in his voice leaves the distinct impression he's native.

This is the first time the French Indian spoke to him from the front row of a city bus. Leroy's eyes spring open to the stare of a college-aged woman from across the aisle. Is it the customary pity and disgust displayed by people who dismiss him as some old drunk? Or is she one of those self-proclaimed old souls who thinks every native elder can turn into an eagle after enough drags on a peace pipe? Leroy wants to yell out that old people of any race get sleepy without booze or drugs or a mystical trance. He can inform her that Leroy Whiskeyjack, PhD, was a big deal back in the day, and that if she'd ever taken a history class, she'd know that.

Leroy says none of those things. He grabs the stainless-steel pole, hoists himself to his feet and yanks the yellow overhead cord. The bus slows to a stop. A hand appears on his shoulder as he turns to the door.

"Professor Whiskeyjack?" the young woman says. "I'm Abigail La Jeune from IPTV. I was hoping to buy you a drink."

Classic technique. Get an old man tipsy so he'd give up his stories. Except Leroy knows he can hold his booze better than this young snot. What is she, twenty, twenty-one? If she's some kind of reporter, she'd be no more than a year out of school. That would put her at twenty-three. The perfect age.

Maybe a drink wouldn't be so bad right now.

"Tell you what," Leroy says. "I know an old pub near here. But the beer's on me."

Little surprise that he nodded off on the bus. Last night, Leroy woke to the all-consuming thought that there was something under his bed. No clue how he knew this; he just did. Is it possible he put it there himself, whatever it was? This thought did nothing to temper the dread creeping up his back, chilling his body, but he resolved to push past it. He swung his legs over the side of the bed and turned on the nightstand lamp.

Leroy leaned in, careful not to lower his head too quickly and initiate another dizzy spell. The dim lighting rewarded his efforts with only a scattering of dust bunnies grazing on the laminate floor under the bed. How could his instincts be so wrong? For all his memory issues, he had never been one for delusions, much less hallucinations. Unless of course there really was something under the goddamned bed.

His eyes cringed as he turned on the overhead lights and sized up his sleeping quarters. For years, he had mused about buying a four-poster oak bed from that Mennonite shoppe up north and turfing the rickety piece of crap he'd bought on sale at Woolworth's back when Woolworth's was still in business. His cheapness appeared to come in handy for once. The particle board bed was much lighter and more portable than solid oak.

The scrape of particle board on laminate reverberated off the sparse décor as he slid the bed toward the wall. Dust bunnies frolicked in the newly disturbed air, all but covering a seam in the middle of the floor. A distinct rectangle interrupted the normal flow of the ten-foot faux wood slats. A trapdoor with only the handle missing.

Leroy lowered himself to the floor, knees creaking. His fingernails traced the seam in the floorboards, lifting the hatchway to reveal the distressed leather equivalent of those inter-office mail envelopes at the university. He unwound a decaying rawhide cord from the pouch.

"Mon Dieu," he exclaimed, reminding himself he didn't speak French.

The folded papers ranged from pale yellow to musty brown. Leroy trusted his instincts and went straight to the brownest and oldest looking of the bunch. The desiccated parchment crackled as he unfolded it. An all-too-familiar cursive leapt from the page despite the age-darkened paper.

> *Urgent note to self:*
>
> Your name is Sosep Atukwet. You were born in the year of our Lord sixteen hundred and seventy-eight. At time of writing, you hold the role of Story Keeper among your people, whom the French mistakenly call the Mik-Mak.
>
> You are confident your band will choose you as leader, which will ease your plan to increase trade with the English. Not everyone will appreciate your efforts, but such is the cost of progress. Or more to the point, profit.
>
> You are reading this because you've reached the age where things slow down and memory fails you. Just a

little longer and you move to the next phase of your existence.

Stay strong!

Sosep

Leroy's eyes could no longer follow the words on the page. Everything around him dissolved—the bedroom walls, the furniture, the crinkled parchment in his hand—the here-and-now consumed by a memory that was clearer than any dream.

Sosep Atukwet's eyes flared through the dimness of his birchbark wikuom.

"I know what you are," he said, "and what you can do."

To the settlers, Atukwet was a great magician, master of the elements who could bend reality to his will. Superstitious nonsense from fishermen and farmers who knew nothing of these things. But it was that very nonsense which made Atukwet's potential so great. He could influence trade with the English, convince the people to cede land and disarm the worthiest adversary with his direct talk. The only antidote to his directness was to match it.

"How could you know what I am? You've only just met me."

"The job of Story Keeper isn't limited to my own people's stories," Atukwet said. "I hear and remember all stories that make their way to our shores. And you, my white-faced friend, are what the Europeans call a shape shifter."

The hiss and snap of the firepit seemed louder than it really was. Talking over them took effort. "Claptrap! Such things do not exist."

"Don't insult me, Monsieur Henri. You know what you've come to do. Kill me and eat my spirit. You'll wear my face and skin like a suit of clothes. My memories will blend with yours until you lose sight of where one of us ends and the other begins. When my essence starts to fade, you will choose another."

"How could you possibly know this?"

Sosep Atukwet stirred the firewood and cast a sidelong glance.

"Nothing magical if that's what you mean. I simply listen for the truth inside every tale. Stories never lie, even when they begin their life as—What was your word?—claptrap."

Firelight glinted off the knife blade as it thrust through the air and into Sosep Atukwet's gut, inches below the breastbone. It tore through skin and fat, cartilage and tendons, pushed with the full force of its bearer's scant body weight. Atukwet's eyes flashed with the light of a Hunter's Moon as a prying hand wrapped around his thrumming heart. The scent of blood wafted from his lips as he gurgled his dying words.

"Why me? All I have are stories."

"Precisely. Your stories are the magic I need."

———

The bartender sets a frosty pint in front of Leroy and draws another for Abigail La Jeune.

"What does Indigenous People's Television want with an old fart like me?" Leroy asks. "Please tell me it's not that claptrap about whether I'm a real Indian."

Abigail thanks the bartender and offers Leroy a broad smile. "I never doubted your claim, Uncle. Between residential schools and the scoop, half your generation is unsure where they were born."

"Thank you," Leroy says. It's been a while since some random native kid called him 'Uncle.' He forgot how it warmed his insides.

"There are some inconsistencies to iron out. This is your opportunity to set the record straight."

Leroy sips his ale and wipes his lips with the back of his hand. "I'd like that."

"Whiskeyjack is not a typical Lakota name. Are you sure your family isn't Cree?"

"I was always told Lakota. There could be some ancestor from North of the Medicine Line."

"There's also the issue of your father," Abigail says. "Pine Ridge has no record of a chief named Whiskeyjack. And no one with Norman as their first name."

Leroy snorts and shakes his head. "Written records only tell half the story. My dad put down his traditional Lakota name as an act of defiance."

Abigail peers over the rims of her glasses. "And what name was that?"

"I don't recall. If you give me a list of Chiefs, I'm sure I could pick it out."

"You don't remember your own dad's traditional name?"

Leroy taps his forehead, blushing. "The old seahorses don't swim like they used to."

"Excuse me?"

"Something my doctor said. Doesn't matter."

Unable to return Abigail's gaze, Leroy sizes up the rows of glasses behind the bar. He notices the obligatory mirror behind the shelf. When a whitish face stares back at him from mirror, his heart starts pounding.

It isn't possible. How could he be showing himself? He isn't that far along yet. Must be some barfly who happens to look like him.

Leroy's head swivels, surveying the empty pub. No one, except Abigail La Jeune and the bartender. When he forces himself to look back at the mirror, his usual reflection greets him, his face startled but intact.

"Are you alright?" Abigail asks. "You look kind of pale."

"I'm fine," Leroy says. "Just overdue for a cigarette."

"I didn't know you smoke."

"There's a lot about me you don't know. If you'd kindly join me outside, there's more I can tell you."

STEP 3: THE SEAHORSES

This is where the tendrils come in. Or more accurately, go in. You pierce the eyeballs, the supple pop awakening your appetites, and it's all you can do not to salivate at the vitreous humor cascading deliciously down the prey's cheeks. You must focus. Now is not the time for gluttony. This step is all about the seahorses.

There are two, one on each side of the brain. If you time it right, they won't remember being taken, the senses having shut down a split second before your tendrils probe into sockets, trailing through twists and turns of fast dying grey matter. They travel and track until they find their targets, attach themselves and absorb as much as they can.

This is when the magic washes over you. There is no more procedure to remember, no conscious task to trouble you. The magic takes care of everything, even the extraneous body lying dead and bloody at your feet. The only thing left is to slip into the current and drift. Swim with the seahorses if you will. And do the one thing you came here to do: You become.

Abigail reclaims her seat at the bar. The bartender looks up from her crossword.

"Another round, hon?"

"Please. Then the check."

"Where's the old native guy?"

"My uncle?" Abigail says. "He retired early."

"Salut," the bartender chimes, setting the ale in front of her.

Abigail slurps the froth from her glass and downs the pint in a single gulp. She wipes her lips with the back of her hand and fishes a notebook from her satchel. Leaning in, she shields the paper from the bartender's view and begins writing.

Urgent note to self:

Your name is Abigail La Jeune. You are of English and Mi'kmaw descent and were born in Newfoundland, Canada, in 2002. You are a distant descendent of Sosep Atukwet, the fabled Mi'kmaw Story Keeper from what the French called Acadie.

At time of writing, you are an intern with Indigenous People's Television. You're investigating the disappearance of noted historian and alleged pretendian Leroy Whiskeyjack. You may not find anything, but your initiative should secure you a full-time position upon graduation.

You are reading this because you've reached the age where things start to slow down, and memory fails you. By now, your name will be the pride of Mi'kmaq everywhere and your words their greatest treasure. Stick to your story, and your next phase of existence will be even better than this one.

All my relations,
Abigail

BAY NAKHT AFN ALTN MARK:
A REHEARSAL

R.B. Lemberg

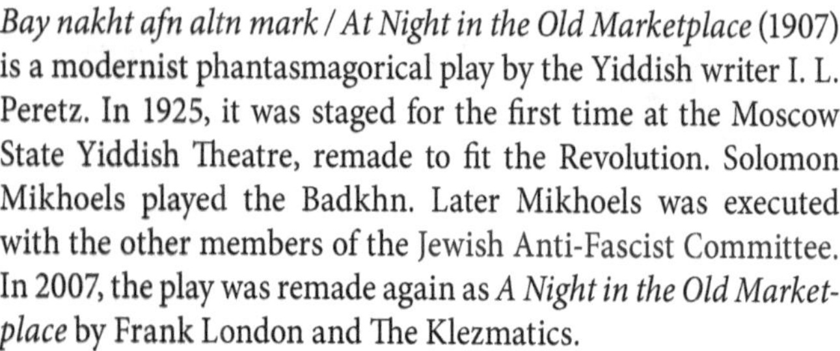

Bay nakht afn altn mark / At Night in the Old Marketplace (1907) is a modernist phantasmagorical play by the Yiddish writer I. L. Peretz. In 1925, it was staged for the first time at the Moscow State Yiddish Theatre, remade to fit the Revolution. Solomon Mikhoels played the Badkhn. Later Mikhoels was executed with the other members of the Jewish Anti-Fascist Committee. In 2007, the play was remade again as *A Night in the Old Marketplace* by Frank London and The Klezmatics.

Something is always missing.

———————

This is a story: there's a marketplace
at midnight. Your voice
calls the dead to awaken.

You'd been a wedding jester here, a Badkhn,
with a tender, slightly mocking cadence
giving the poor bride to the rich groom,
a merchant.
She wanted someone else,
someone younger, rosy-cheeked, but you joked
you lamented
     you told off-color parables to the guests:
  and, so the story goes, she fled,
threw herself into the well
     in the middle of the marketplace.
The merchant—well, he got himself a bear,
became a recluse. That rosy-cheeked fool

of a lover of hers—
        he drank himself to redness.

This is not a story: kaleidoscopic.
Dancers, sex workers, revolutionaries, merchants,
Kabbalists, Cossacks, undoubtedly somewhere a goat
nibbling on the roof; it would eat the moon, too, and
standing on the roof, the goat
would play the violin, but the singers
of Brod, one with his own violin, another with a red banner,
have scared the goat away. A house of study.
The moon clutches
the town to its translucent bosom.
You dream of revolutions
and dust; you dream
of your own story.

This is a story: you regret
her death.
        Regret
outweighs the moon and all the goats that dance on it.
You blow the night watchman's whistle;
the sounds of the shofar—
t'kiah—
t'ruah—
t'kiah—
   mix with the wedding melody.
Above the town, where once there was a moon,
a cemetery now hangs in midair.
The mechanical rooster
turns. The dead
begin to spill out of their graves.

Sheyndele, too cold for any wedding,
has arisen
from her well.

This is not a story: a Recluse with his bear.
He once was a merchant, successful, tall,
bearded, in a tailored kaftan,
        married—almost—
but she wanted someone else. Anyone
else: blood, rifles,
the nuptial kiss of water: anything.

The bridegroom—
he, too, was reluctant.
That's a different story.

This is not a story: There is no resolution
but the Word. And bird:
the mechanical rooster
in a town of fragments.

There is no resolution
but this kaleidoscope
of forgettings, and then questions:
words, awaiting
that single Word. An order. An ordaining.
Waiting—forever, it seems.

This is a story: somewhere above the town
dead Sheyndele and her drunk fool
dance under the black canopy
in the cemetery in the sky.

But you—the wedding jester—are not there.
You're wondering about the bear.
There hasn't been a bear
    before. This is the grand rehearsal
            of a play that's never been performed
                    as written (or even fully written: always changing).
There is a further

disintegration in this, a story that collapses
into itself like a burning Torah scroll
into ash, like regret
into a well, like revolutions
into murders, like a hand motioning
downwards—
     Ah. That was you,
trying to take a different tack. *"Go back—"*
   you cry, and the cemetery
vanishes.
The bride returns to dust, her drunk beloved
fast asleep under the gibbous moon.
You are still here—a Badkhn with no wedding.
no canopy: not for the living or the dead,
no roof. No town. No banner,
no promise of a brighter time;
no wedding klezmer.

The Recluse hangs around.

Tell me a parable—
he says. His voice scrapes low
    at the white moon-gate of the garden of the night:
tell me a riddle,
a divination,
a secret.

He, too, had hidden things. One must
become a recluse
to conceal a bear
    and all that goes with it.

This is a story: this is always the story,
but just queering it is not enough
   to ease the sheer impossibility of history
 or even change much,

if you're honest with yourself—
because the tale undoes all moods except this one.
The no-escape. The crushing melancholy.

It swallows all—
    the living and the dead,
    each time the moon, and all the revolutions,
    the stage set with its rooster, and the town,
and all the losses and regrets:
even itself;

even the hidden Word.

The Recluse says,
    Tell me a story which is not a story.
You say,
    Ask me a question from this silence.

You'll try again.
You'll tell and you'll untell this one
    —no jest—
under a different canopy
            (sometimes it's yours)
    in each disjointed time and tangled way,
until a tiny bit, however small, is mended
    of this devoured, despairing world

and maybe not alone
and maybe even now

Fiction

PUNKS DON'T DIE

Kat Sedia

THE LAST TIME I saw Stepan was at St. Petersburg Central Station. I was hanging out of the window of the Red Arrow express train, kissing Stepan who was on the platform, doing his best to squeeze as much affection as possible from these last few minutes. Mitya, sighing and rolling his eyes, held onto the waist of my jeans to prevent me from falling onto the platform teeth first.

"The train is about to leave," a very tired engineer said over the speaker. "As soon as the girl in the seventh car stops dangling out of the window. Let him go, honey, I'm sure they have dick in Moscow."

"That's you," Mitya said, unnecessarily, and pulled me into the car. "It'll be fine, you'll see him in two days."

He was wrong on both counts.

———

Stepan comes to me in a dream, sullen, with a bleeding lower lip split just where his lower canine has been knocked out. He's wearing a black T-shirt as always, so I don't notice the blood soaking it right away, and only feel the bone knife handle under his ribs when I hold him.

"Fuck," I say, with the calmness of my dream self, "what happened to you?"

"Got fucked," he says. "Got a smoke?"

We are sitting on my dorm bed, and I watch him blowing smoke out of his nostrils, a twin dragon exhale. "Do you think the world deserves to exist?" Stepan asks.

"No," I answer with the conviction I rarely feel when I am awake. "Are you dead?"

His stupid snorting laugh sounds real enough. "No," he says. "Are you high? Let's get drunk and go fuck on the roof."

I point at the knife handle, and he touches it. "Huh," he says. "It's like…I can't move it. It's fused to me."

"We can fuck anyway," I say.

He kneels between my thighs and leans over me for a kiss. His mouth tastes like blood, and I wake up.

On the train, Mitya wouldn't let up. He was ten years older, and knew me my entire life—he was best friends with my brother Anton since first grade. And when Anton came back from Afghanistan in a steel coffin, Mitya took it upon himself to fulfill the duties of an older brother as he understood them—including tracking me down in St. Petersburg and bringing me to Moscow where the university exam session was about to start.

"I have a wife and a child," Mitya said. "I don't need this. The farmer who had no troubles just had to buy a pig, as they say."

"Nobody asked you to."

He sighed, stretched out his legs across the space between our seats. "Zhenya, believe me, I know. I watched you do every stupid thing I myself had done, and I told you in advance how stupid it was, but of course you had to try everything yourself. But please don't drop out of school."

I stared out of the window, watching the new high-rises on the outskirts of St. Petersburg fly by. Of course Mitya was correct; it just didn't particularly help at that moment, when leaving Stepan behind felt like an amputation.

"I am not even going to ask you what you see in that guy," Mitya said. "Date whoever, punks, hippies, gopniks, I don't care. But none of them are worth dropping out for."

He stared out of the window too, and I tried imagining Anton's round babyface, which I would've forgotten by now if it wasn't for photos, superimposed on Mitya's bearded visage, reminiscent of early saints—a similarity of which he was aware, and cultivated. Mitya was an artist, and he had an exhibit coming up, and he really didn't need my shit. I wished he would just give up and let me be, while also realizing that left to my own devices I would make some regrettable choices.

Mitya rose and went to have a smoke in the gangway. I followed.

"You mad?" I asked after he offered me his pack, silently.

"A little," he said. "I feel like I always have to claw you away from some degenerate who's trying to drag you down."

I leaned against the clanging, shuddering wall—it felt like a hide of a magical beast, rasping and roaring. "Not down," I said. "I'm already down. He is dragging me closer."

———

The first time I saw Stepan was two years ago, outside of a bar near the Kazan Cathedral. To be accurate, I didn't see him—just four guys in tracksuits kicking someone on the ground. When I got closer, I saw a punk kid about my age and was immediately shaken by the fact that instead of curling up into a fetal position as most of us would, he still struggled to get up, and screamed insults at his attackers through split lips.

"Guys," I tried, but they were not listening.

I threw myself onto the kid on the ground, like a war hero onto a hand grenade, hoping that whatever vestiges of chivalry these gopniks had would prevent them from kicking a lady.

"Fuck it," one of them said.

I was never sure how soon they left—I was so distracted by staring into Stepan's one visible eye (the other was swollen shut), blue and deep like Lake Baikal. I wouldn't know what he really looked like for weeks, his face was so bruised. But that eye…

He stared back, silent.

"We should probably get up," I said, and felt him get hard under me. "You need stitches too. Is there a clinic nearby?"

"Uh-huh," he said, and put his undamaged hand on my back. "Who are you, and do you fuck?"

I watched the doctor stitch up his lip and split eyebrow. The doctor was middle-aged, heavy, very sweet. "Keep him out of trouble," he told me. "I've been seeing a lot of…untraditional young men lately."

"Gopniks were picking on him," I said. "Fucking wastes of air."

Stepan took offense. "I was picking on them," he said. "For being such pieces of shit."

The doctor finished sewing him up. "Maybe keep yourself out of trouble then," he told me.

Stepan lived nowhere in particular. There was a squat where he slept periodically, and he had civilian friends who would let him crash on their couches if he asked. Once, a friend of his was out of town for a weekend and left Stepan the keys, and in those two days he was outside of me for maybe fifteen minutes when he went out to get cigarettes.

The swelling in his face was gone by then, and he was beautiful in a disreputable way, but that's not why I was so in love with him.

———

Stepan comes to me in a dream. We are in a park, in Moscow somewhere—maybe Tsaritsyno. We are walking hand in hand, and Stepan is drunk and more talkative than usual. "Zhenya," he says, "I love you so much. Like if love was an explosive, I would probably have enough to blow up the whole world."

I laugh. "I love you too. Does it hurt?" I point at the bone handle of the knife that seems to be growing a bit dry and desiccated.

He shakes his head and puts his arm around my neck and pulls me close to him; I try to avoid the knife handle as I put my arm around his waist, and feel his T-shirt, wet and sticky and fetid with blood. We walk along a poplar-lined alley, shaded and silent, and it doesn't look like this alley will ever end.

———

"Have you ever been in a psychiatric hospital?" Stepan asked me one day—it was soon after we first met, before we ever were apart again. We had nowhere to be, so we went for a walk, and to drink canned gin and tonics by the Neva.

"Yeah," I said. "A few times."

"Me too." He looked at the water, leaden and lazy. It must've been early September, since it was still warm enough for him to wear just a windbreaker over his T-shirt. "Promise me something."

"What?"

"If they ever put you away again…don't take their pills, don't let them do any motherfucking therapy on you." His voice shook just a little. "Don't put up with any of that bullshit."

"Why would I start now?"

He grabbed my hand and pulled me into his arms. We kissed furiously, as if there was something threatening to tear us away from each other. He told me that he came to St. Petersburg from Rostov, to apply to the Pavlov's Medical Institute, but ended up in a psychiatric hospital after a particularly violent and uneven altercation. He emerged a few months later with a finely honed understanding of the world, and the only medicine he was interested in after that was therapeutic blood-letting via street fights.

When nights grew colder, he forced the lock on the basement boiler room in an old Krushchev-built apartment building, and we stayed there until late September, when I regretfully had to admit that I needed to go back to Moscow since my first year of the university started some weeks ago, without my participation.

"It's okay," Stepan said. "I'll come visit you."

He traveled using the time-honored method of hippies and demobilized soldiers—riding local trains all the way from St. Petersburg to Moscow, switching at the end of the lines, avoiding conductors by running ahead of them or jumping up on the luggage shelves and waiting them out, because in those years no one ever looked up. It took anywhere between six and ten trains—depending on how proficient the conductors were—and cost nothing. I could always feel him getting closer across those 635 kilometers, by the pull on my heart and the thudding of the trains in my ears, until the whistles and clanging became a steady roar and the security guard knocked on my door asking if I knew this guy. And Stepan would be there, smiling, built like a German shepherd puppy with his long limbs and large hands and feet he would never get a chance to fully grow into.

And then it quieted down, as the screaming of my blood in my ears subsided, and we kissed and fucked and talked, Stepan inarticulately brilliant, as he always struggled to explain things he knew deep in his bones, until the struggle became too much and he slammed his head against the wall and went out to get fucked up and fucked over.

———

Stepan comes to me in a dream. The bone handle looks withered like an umbilical cord on a day-old kitten, and the poplar alley has finally ended and is giving way to a lush meadow, the kind only possible where rivers are fed with snowmelt and overflow their banks every spring. I tell him about how back home we used to take boats to rescue stranded animals during spring floods, and about a badger who scratched me at first but then settled down and just watched me, judgmental of my handling of the oars.

"If I die," Stepan says, with emphasis on *if,* "where do you think I'll go?"

"Valhalla," I answer. "I mean, assuming you die in battle."

He carefully fingers the withered knife handle. "Yeah. But I don't think you should go with me."

"I'll walk you partway."

Our fingers entwine so hard it hurts. It is always bone-on-bone with him, ribs on ribs, femur on femur. Our bodies lack the most basic defenses against each other, and the more we love the more we cut.

We walk across the lush meadow that looks like it will never end. The sun above us is gray and the grass looks black in this light, whispering under our feet.

———

Mitya came to visit soon after the exams were over. It was real spring by then; the air was still blue and thick at 10 p.m., and you could smell the lilacs all the way up on the fourth floor of the dorm.

"How did you do?" he asked.

"Fine. I passed everything. Qualified for the stipend, even."

He breathes a huge sigh of relief. "Zhenya, I don't tell you this enough but you are really smart. Anyone dumber would've failed out already, you fuck around so much. And now just two more years."

"How was your exhibit?" I asked. "I went Wednesday, it seemed really well-attended."

"It's good." He sighed. "You know how it is—what I like and what everyone else likes don't overlap."

I knew what he meant; I liked his abstract stuff too, but the exhibit was all paintings of churches and Slavic aesthetics that became suddenly popular. "You do have a child to feed."

He lit up a cigarette and offered me one too. "Thanks for not calling me a sellout."

"At least they're buying. Nothing sadder than selling out for free."

He smiled then. "Good point. Yeah, I sold like fifteen large pieces. And I also got you something…in case you didn't fail out."

He pulled a thin folder out of his bag. It was a pencil sketch of Stepan, sitting in his habitual crouch, long arms dangling over his knees, smiling. Just a few quick lines managed to capture him so perfectly that my mouth went dry with longing. I also couldn't miss the clear affection that went into this drawing.

"You like him," I said. "Thanks."

"How is he? I thought he'd be here."

I shook my head. "He's dead, Mitya."

———

Mitya met Stepan one of the first times he came to Moscow. We were drinking beer in bed, and when Mitya knocked on the door we scrambled to get at least partially dressed.

"Who are you?" Stepan asked, sizing up Mitya. His hand grasped the neck of the empty beer bottle habitually.

"An artist," I said, just as Mitya said, "Her brother."

"Self-appointed," I clarified, "but yeah. Stepan, don't start shit."

Stepan studied Mitya and his blue-and-white striped shirt, the kind sailors usually wear, and that was popular with certain St. Petersburg bohemians. "You're from Peter?"

"No," Mitya said. "But I was a paratrooper. More importantly, who are you?"

"This is Stepan," I said. "Mitya, don't you start either. Want a beer?"

"Okay." He settled on the chair by my desk and studied Stepan some more.

Stepan wasn't wearing a shirt, so long violet bruises on his ribs were starkly visible, and he stared back, defiantly.

I pulled on my jeans and went to the fridge in the shared kitchen to get a Baltika 4 for Mitya.

I came back to Mitya in his full brotherly gopnik mode. "And what do you do? I mean besides having shit kicked out of you."

Stepan shrugged. "I sometimes unload trucks, liquor stores mostly."

"Of course. Ever took anything that didn't belong to you?"

"If it wasn't nailed down. Oh, and a bunch of my friends are musicians, so I help with equipment. My arms are long enough to carry two amps at once. So I get paid sometimes."

"That's very impressive," Mitya said with less venom than I expected, and took the beer. "Do your parents know where you are?"

Stepan shrugged again. "We don't talk. But I am nineteen, so it doesn't matter."

"Not worried about the conscription?"

"Nah. Exempt on psychiatric grounds."

Mitya always had very expressive eyes, so he managed to telegraph his disappointment at me while drinking his beer. "All right," he told me. "I have a newborn at home, I have to go." He then nodded at Stepan. "I don't care what you do, but if there's any collateral damage to her, I will gut you like a fish."

"No shit, bro." Stepan reached out his hand. "I'll die before I put her in harm's way."

Mitya considered but shook the offered hand. "I'll see you around, bro. Don't burn up, okay?"

———

After the meadow, there is a forest. It doesn't look like any real place anymore—the trees are all bare, craggy branches, twisting themselves into the black sky. There's the barest dusting of stars but it's not dark, just dim. There is nothing alive around us, and we both shiver but continue walking, our arms around each other for warmth. The bone handle of the knife is nothing but a rough bump under his sticky T-shirt.

"Shit," he says. "I am really sorry."

"No, I am sorry. I knew I shouldn't have left you."

He laughs. "I am not a baby."

"Yeah, you're just a fuckup."

"Yeah." He stops and turns me toward him, and bends down to kiss me. That's what he does when words fail him, as they regularly do. Affection and self-harm are the only things he is capable of, and his arms are the awkward crossroads between the two. "It really fucking hurts," he says, and I know that he doesn't mean the blade, and I wonder if that's withering too, or growing sharper inside of him.

———

Mitya took the news harder than I expected. He sobbed for a good long while, his hand over his eyes. He didn't have to say it, I understood that it wasn't just Stepan—but also Anton, and Mitya himself, and me. If I still had the capacity, I would've cried too, because of how random it was that Mitya was alive and not Anton, and how stupid it was of him to make me his atonement project.

Instead I got us beers, and we drank and smoked, the window open into the cooling night.

"Fuck," Mitya said. "Sorry for losing my shit like this...I live with my wife, my mom, and two sisters, it's like a sea of estrogen over there."

"Sure, blame the women."

He smiled a bit. "What else am I going to do? Plus you, here. Will you be okay?"

I wanted to tell him about how Stepan visited me in my dreams, about our long and cold walk, about how real he felt. Instead I said, "What else am I going to do?"

He sighed. "Why are you kids like this?"

I gestured with my cigarette at the window, at the world outside. "Rapidly contracting horizons, I guess."

Mitya finished his beer. "You know, when I was your age, I was madly in love with this girl. On nights like this, we would be just walking around, for hours, just talking about everything."

"And what happened to her?"

"Fell out of love."

"It's a good night for being outside. Come on, I'll walk you to the subway."

The grounds around the dorms were thick with couples, and as we turned to the boulevard, even more of them sat on benches. May was always like that.

"Fuck," Mitya said. "Life goes by too fast."

"You're barely thirty."

"And it's not going to slow down from this point on." He squeezed my elbow. "You sure you're okay?"

"I won't end up in Kashchenko again, if that's what you're asking."

"Good. I don't ever want to find you in a pool of your own blood again."

"Someone else's blood is okay though."

He laughed. "Better them than us."

We stopped in front of the subway station. "Thanks, Mitya," I said. "Don't worry so much."

"Well, with you I don't think I have a choice. Just call if things go south."

"I promise."

———

I find Stepan waiting for me at the edge of the forest. He nods wordlessly, his sharp chin pointing at something ahead. We walk onto the riverbank hand in hand, and walk along the embankment, and gray granite becomes white sand under our feet, the leaden waters of the Neva turn into the Styx or whatever underworld river Stepan needs to cross.

He stands by the water, looking into the darkened air, listening to something I cannot yet hear. I sit on the sand, watching him, the silhouette my eyes learned to snatch from any crowd, any mosh pit, any street fight. Wide shoulders, the edge of unevenly chopped off T-shirt sleeves, hips cocked, his weight on one leg, always ready to leap into whatever melee presented itself. Already untethered from the world and barely tethered to me.

"It's a nice place," I say.

He turns around and sits next to me. "It is. I wonder what's on the other side."

"I don't think I can come there with you."

"Yeah." He thinks. "I could stay here though. For a bit, you know."

"I could come and visit."

"I mean, that's what we've been doing anyway. I wonder how long we can last."

I laugh. "Like that time you put novocaine on your dick."

He laughs too. "No, I mean, here. How long I can wait, how long you can visit."

I rest my head against his shoulder. "Until one of us gets tired. You know one of us will."

He wraps his arm around my shoulders. "It always happens. But not yet."

The water is thick and black, and finally, finally I hear the splashing and creaking of oars, and I wonder if that's how that stupid badger felt watching our boat grow solid out of the mist.

NOT A BIRD

Ellen Romano

My friend's dead father
visits her as a bird,

but my husband is the light in the kitchen
that comes on all by himself,

and I see I've written *himself*
instead of *itself.* Just when I'd decided

to call an electrician and stop talking
to the dead and gone

there he is on the page,
Howard himself,

and the light still burns.

Fiction

LIMINALITIES OF THE SECOND CONTRACTION
Scott Payne

I. RUINED

The dome's interior is an endless summer sky. The eye is lured downward from the bright, cloudless horizon to the swaying bustle of wheat. The interminable fields themselves are intersected with soft, grassy paths, just wide enough for two to walk hand in hand. Merely by looking at the natural splendor rendered in vibrant blue, gold, and green, one could almost feel the welcome radiance of warm sunlight upon their skin.

The panorama's seemingly boundless dimensions—its joyful openness—collapses only when the hole intrudes upon one's vision. It appears like a circular splotch of black paint just above the miniscule, trembling heads of the lifelike wheat at the horizon. Dark, irregular cracks spread outward from the hole like seeking roots, penetrating the otherwise perfectly azure sky.

The hole belies the artificially eternal proportions of the sky and fields, cruelly collapsing the illusion that one is outside and free. If one turns their back on it, they are immersed in a ceaseless horizon stretching out before them, awash in bright, terrestrial grandeur. But facing the hole, the beholder is forced to register the cramped dimensions of the dome, the smallness and utter falseness of the scene, no matter how picturesque it may be. An open world becomes a broken screen.

Anybody gazing into the hole would soon discern that it is not perfectly black, as it may first appear. From time to time the soft gleam of a distant star revolves slowly through this unwelcome portal to the outer dark. The tips of wheat, though still made to sway and whisper pleasantly with a nonexistent breeze, are covered with barely perceptible frost. The summer's warmth that once gently exuded from the inviting, soft soil has long since radiated out through the hole. Now the bright, sunny day is forever grasped by the invisible cold of infinite space.

II. ABANDONED

The blue light slowly strobes, forming a small, delicate orb of visibility about the dormant station before gradually relenting to the insistent darkness of the surrounding sea. At the light's nadir, there is brief moment of utter blackness before the glow returns once more to press futilely against the liquid void.

Endless waters stretch above, below, about the motionless station suspended in the benthic gloom. There is no visible marker to indicate the station's bearings or even its orientation. It is impossible to tell in which direction sits the icebound surface or the barren seafloor, each unseen boundary being so unutterably distant as to be imaginary.

The station is composed of two bulges of thick glass connected by a short, opaque corridor. At the height of the blue light's strobing, had some swimmer just outside the station been able to withstand the crushing deep, they would be able to peer through the glass and make out the bare traces of long-disused chairs, metallic instrument panels, food trays set in jumbled disorder.

There is no marine snow to flit past the station, no life to be revealed by the blue glow. The light illuminates only invisible waters. There will never be anything here but the slow waxing and waning of this light. For as long as the station retains power, the scene will be unchangeable, a perfectly recreated cycle of the paltry light's growth and retreat. But when the light finally fails, long centuries from now, there will once more be no sanctuary from the absolute darkness of the currentless sea.

III. EMPTIED

Floating above the ice, the burgundy spacesuit is like a tiny drop of blood on the immense, broken skin of the moon. Were it not for the suit's weightlessness, it would be possible to tell whether or not a body, living or dead, lies within it. But the suit has long been bereft of its former inhabitants.

The suit slumps forward in an attitude of resignation, arms raised slightly and preceding the gentle course of the body. Its golden faceplate reflects the slow trawl of blue-tinged chasms and crevasses as it steadily traverses the moon. The suit bears an antique momentum that will never abate, endlessly surveying the depths and rises of the icy expanse beneath it.

The detritus of a frenzied evacuation carried out centuries ago still floats above the suit in invisible stratifications. Blankets, handheld tools, and freeze-dried food packages trace their own sluggish orbits above the ice. Their tiny shadows sail unseen across the moon's surface, speckling the frozen wasteland.

Solitary witness to the fragmented moon, the spacesuit is variously and irregularly encrusted with the ice-spray of cryo-volcanoes and gently thawed by the feeble rays of the distant sun. Its faceplate will gaze upon every inch of the surface many times over before the kin of its long-absent occupants may return. Meanwhile, it silently haunts this broken, vacant world.

IV. UNFINISHED

The silvery steps gleam harshly with the reflected light of the sun's rise, an incongruous glare among the dull, dusty beige. They stand alone atop a plateau of rough-hewn, craggy rock. Each of the twelve steps is slightly narrower than the last, rising grandly upward and cutting into the soft black airlessness above.

As the sun passes in its course, the steps' shadow expands and twists itself into an immense pyramid before dwindling into a thin, snakelike line. The meandering black inscribes itself into the indifferent dust and rock of the plateau before the light quits the surface. As the sun retires, the stairs are slowly bled of their splendor, blending into the small, leaden mesa about them.

It will never be remembered what absent monument or shrine these steps were meant to convey the moon's pilgrims to. The stairway itself remains untrodden and forgotten, leading to nothing. And yet every few years, from the perspective of the first broad and shining step, the stairs' zenith will perfectly frame the tilted visage of Saturn. It is as though, in this brief moment, one could mount these bright steps and effortlessly ascend, godlike, to take their place upon the ringed throne.

AUTHOR BIOS

MALENA SALAZAR MACIÁ is the author of the novels *La ira de los sobrevivientes*, *Aliento de Dragón*, and *Los errantes*, among others. Her texts have been collected in both national and foreign anthologies. English translations of her stories have appeared in *Clarkesworld*, *Strange Horizons*, and *Dark Matter Magazine*. Her work has also been translated into Croatian, German, Italian, and Japanese.

BELLE BISCOTTI is a young poet/writer from Down Under who enjoys writing horror and science fiction. She wrote this poem as an homage to mushrooms. Her work has appeared in *The Village Observer*.

TEMIDAYO TESTIMONY OMALI ODEY, also known as Testimony Odey, is a Nigerian multidisciplinary artist exploring the intersections of literature, film, spoken word, and music. With publications in several magazines, she has been shortlisted for the African Human Rights Short Story Prize, the Brigitte Poirson Literature Prize, and the global Writing Ukraine Prize, and is a recipient of the Nigeria Prize for Teen Authors, an African Teen Writers Award, the HIASFEST Star Prize, the Wakaso Poetry Prize, and a JCIN UNIBEN Ten Emerging Leaders and Legacy Award. When she's not creating, she is either reading, watching a film, or spinning philosophical theories in her head.

SHANA ROSS is a recent transplant to Edmonton, Alberta, and Treaty Six Territory. Qui transtulit sustinet. Her work has recently appeared in *Haven Spec, Identity Theory, Ninth Letter, The Dread Machine,* and more. She is the winner of the 2022 Anne C. Barnhill Prize and the 2021 Bacopa Literary Review Poetry competition. She serves as an editor for *Luna Station Quarterly* and a critic for *Pencilhouse.* She prefers walking in the woods to social media, so she budgets her time accordingly.

ERIN ULM is an undergraduate student at Southern Oregon University in Ashland, Oregon. Between classes, she writes speculative fiction short stories.

MATTHEW WOLLIN is a writer, filmmaker, and lawyer. His journalism has appeared in *Mother Jones, Newsweek,* and *Slate,* and his creative work in *Nightmare Magazine, Amazing Stories, juked,* and elsewhere. His speculative memoir-in-progress was a finalist for the Iowa Short Fiction Award and a semifinalist for the University of New Orleans Publishing Lab Prize. *The Hollywood Reporter* called him "a talent to watch" for his debut feature film as writer/director, *The Skin of the Teeth.* You can read more of his work on his Substack, "Should You Care?" or on his website at matthewwollin.com.

LAILA AMADO is a nomadic writer of (mostly) short fiction. She writes in her second language, has recently exchanged her fourth country of residence for the fifth, and can now be found staring at the North Sea, instead of the Mediterranean. The sea, occasionally, stares back. Follow her on Bluesky @amadolaila.bsky.social.

JASON PEARCE is an Ontario-based writer of literary and speculative fiction, exploring themes of Indigenous cultural identity, language loss, and rural life. His work has appeared in a variety of magazines and anthologies, including *Flash Fiction Online, Grain, Solstice in Purgatory,* and *Knucklehead Noir.* A proud alumnus of the Audible Indigenous Writers' Circle, Jason is of English and Mi'kmaw descent.

R.B. LEMBERG (they/them) is a queer, bigender immigrant from Ukraine to the US. R.B. is an author of six books of speculative fiction and poetry, an academic, and a translator from Ukrainian and Russian. R.B.'s work has been shortlisted for the Le Guin Prize for Fiction, Nebula, Locus, Ignyte, World Fantasy, and other awards. You can find R.B. on Instagram @rblemberg, Bluesky @rblemberg.bsky.social, and at their website rblemberg.net.

KAT SEDIA is a critically acclaimed writer of speculative fiction and noir, and a World Fantasy Award–winning editor. Their novel *The Alchemy of Stone* was nominated for the Otherwise Award, and *Heart of Iron* was shortlisted for the Sidewise Award. Their short story collection, *Moscow But Dreaming*, featured a number of their short stories originally published in venues such as *Asimov's*, *Analog*, *Clarkesworld*, and several anthologies. Kat currently resides in the Pinelands of New Jersey, where they teach biology at a state university and run a rescue for medically needy cats. They are a communist, an abolitionist, and support free Palestine and Land Back.

ELLEN ROMANO is a retired educator and widow living in Hayward, California, where she enjoys frequent visits with her children and grandchildren. She is the winner of Third Wednesday's 2023 Poetry Prize, Ink Nest Poem of the Month, and several awards from the Ina Coolbrith Circle. Other work has appeared in *Lascaux Review*, *december magazine*, *Naugatuck River Review*, and other publications.

SCOTT PAYNE (he/him) is a lawyer and history nerd from Vancouver, British Columbia. He has short stories published and forthcoming with *The Deadlands*, *Neon & Smoke*, *Queen's Quarterly*, and *Twenty Two Twenty Eight*.

STAFF BIOS

SEAN MARKEY publishes websites for a living and has always dreamed of starting a publishing company (about Death). He lives with his wife, Beth, and a handful of well-traveled pets, in northwest Spain.

E. CATHERINE TOBLER is a writer and editor. You might know her editing work from *Shimmer Magazine*. You might know her writing from *Clarkesworld, Lightspeed*, and *Apex Magazine*. A trebuchet and Oxford comma enthusiast, she enjoys gelato and beer in her free time. Leo sun, Taurus moon. You can find her on Bluesky @ecatherine.com.

NICASIO ANDRES REED is a writer, poet, and essayist whose work has appeared in venues such as *Shimmer, Fireside, Lightspeed,* and *Uncanny Magazine*. He's read slush for *Strange Horizons,* edited manuscripts for award-winning authors, and owns five different copies of *Moby Dick*. He lives with his family in Cavite province in the Philippines.

INKSHARK is a scandalously queer illustrator, author, and editor who lives in the rainy wilds of the Pacific Northwest. He enjoys exploring with his dogs, writing impossible things, and painting what he shouldn't. When his current meatshell begins to decay, he'd like science to put his brain into a giant killer octopus body with which he promises to be responsible and not even slightly shipwrecky. Pinky swear.

DAVID GILMORE is a writer, reader, and editor out of St. Louis, MO. His work has been featured in *The Rumpus* and at Lindenwood University, where he also received his MFA. He lives with his family and spends his free time manning a stall in the Goblin Market selling directions to various Underworlds in exchange for rumors and information on where he can find his muse.

AMANDA DOWNUM is the author of *The Necromancer Chronicles, Dreams of Shreds & Tatters,* and the World Fantasy Award–nominated collection *Still So Strange.* Not content with armchair necromancy, she is also a licensed mortician. She lives in Austin, TX, with an invisible cat. You can summon her at a crossroads at midnight on the night of a new moon, or find her on Bluesky as @stillsostrange.

LAURA BLACKWELL is a freelance copy editor and Shirley Jackson Award–winning writer. Her publications include stories in *Chiral Mad 5, Nightmare,* and the 2023 Shirley Jackson Award winner *Aseptic and Faintly Sadistic: An Anthology of Hysteria Fiction.* Visit her website—and if you like, sign up for her newsletter—at pronouncedlahra.com.

CHRISTINE M. SCOTT has been a professional graphic designer, website developer, and brand consultant for more than thirty years. She is the creative director and copublisher of Nosetouch Press and has coedited seven anthologies, including the folk horror anthology trilogy *The Fiends in the Furrows.* She is also an artist and craftsperson—several of her handcrafted items were included in *Game of Thrones: The Compendium,* printed by Chronicle Books for HBO. For a complete list of her pursuits, please visit christinemariescott.com.

FELICIA MARTÍNEZ is a writer and artist born and raised in Eastern New Mexico, though home is now the San Francisco Bay Area. She is a 2023 Dream Foundry Contest for Emerging Writers finalist, an honor she achieved with a beloved work of flash. Find her on Bluesky and Instagram as @feliciafm.

ANNIKA BARRANTI KLEIN is a freelance editor with a writing habit. Her work can be found at annikaobscura.com. She is supervised by a cat at all times.

www.ingramcontent.com/pod-product-compliance
Lightning Source LLC
Chambersburg PA
CBHW030011010826
48973CB00009B/2764